DEFENDER
DRAGON

DEFENDER DRAGON

PROTECTION, INC.
2

ZOE CHANT

AUTHOR'S NOTE

This book stands alone. However, it's the second in a series about an all-shifter private security agency, Protection, Inc. If you'd like to read the series in order, the first book is *Bodyguard Bear*, the third is *Protector Panther*, and the fourth is *Warrior Wolf*.

TABLE OF CONTENTS

CHAPTER ONE
Lucas

Tick-tock.

Usually Lucas enjoyed the ticking of the antique grandfather clock in the meeting room of Protection, Inc. So many things in America were so new that they seemed cheap and sterile. But Hal Brennan, the huge bear shifter who ran the private security company, had a taste for the old and cozy. Hence, the clock of wood and brass.

But today the ticking was driving Lucas crazy. He wished Hal had been more of a typical American and furnished the room with a silent digital clock. Then Lucas could have simply not looked at it.

It was time for the weekly meeting, when all seven members of Protection, Inc. reported on their cases, but Lucas was the only one there. He glanced at the clock again to see if he was early, but he was exactly on time.

"I said, 'Where is everyone?'" Nick's voice, raised and rough with annoyance, startled Lucas. He'd been so distracted, he hadn't seen Nick come in.

Lucas covered up his inattention with an icy stare. Nick scowled, his tattooed arms folded across his chest and his wolf glaring right back at Lucas from behind the man's green eyes.

"I don't know," Lucas admitted. "It's late—they're late."

No. I'm late, he thought. *I'm too late. Today is the last day. If I don't find my mate today, it's all over.*

Tick-tock.

Hal threw open the door. He held a blood-soaked cloth to his head. His shirt was torn, exposing the bulletproof vest beneath.

Lucas started up from his seat. "Hal! You're hurt."

"It's nothing." Hal looked more embarrassed than pained.

His curvy mate, Ellie, followed close behind him, a first aid kit in her hand. "Hal, sit down and let me examine you."

Hal's rugged features softened into a smile. "Sure. I'm all yours."

He sprawled out in the huge leather chair that had been custom-made for his larger-than-life size. Ellie, who was a paramedic, sat beside him and took his pulse.

"I appreciate you calling me," Ellie said softly.

Hal ruffled her hair. "No one but you gets to patch me up."

The intimacy between them made Lucas feel his ever-present loneliness even more sharply. What must it be like to have a mate? Could that bond of love warm even the frozen places inside of him?

The rest of the members of Protection, Inc. filed into the room. From their chatter, they had run into Hal in the parking lot on their way to the meeting.

Rafa, the lion shifter, leaned over the table, his black hair falling over the anxious creases in his forehead. He and Hal had been Navy SEALs together before Hal had founded Protection, Inc.

"Hal—" Rafa broke off, shaking his head ruefully. "No, wait, you'll say you're fine no matter what. Ellie, *is* he all right?"

"Yes, he actually is. It's a shallow cut, but any wound to the head bleeds a lot. I'll just put in a few stitches so it doesn't scar." Ellie applied antiseptic to a cloth pad and began to clean the cut.

"How'd you get clocked?" Destiny asked, dumping her backpack and skateboard on the floor.

Lucas was amused to see that she and Fiona had come straight from their undercover assignment at a local high school. Fiona was primly dressed as a teacher, her blonde hair pinned into a bun and glasses she didn't need perched on her elegant nose, while curvy Destiny was impersonating a student in cut-off shorts and light-up sneakers.

"I was fighting three guys, and number four snuck up behind me," Hal replied.

"Careless," Shane remarked, making Lucas jump. The quiet panther shifter had managed to sit down next to him without him noticing. At least that wasn't due to Lucas being distracted; Shane could sneak up on anyone.

Hal shrugged, then winced as the movement pulled at the stitch Ellie was putting in. "They're all in jail now. Job done. Okay, guys. Report."

Normally Lucas paid close attention at team meetings. Though his country, Brandusa, had an elected parliament, the royal family still had a substantial amount of power. As the crown prince, he had been raised from childhood to sit through excruciatingly boring, six-hour conferences on taxes and treaties. And then he'd been quizzed on them. Protection, Inc. meetings were no trouble compared to that. Usually he enjoyed hearing everyone's accounts of protection and adventure.

But despite his training and the exciting stories everyone was telling, his attention drifted. By the end of the day, unless a miracle occurred, he'd be summoned back to Brandusa. Forever.

Tick-tock.

Hal cleared his throat. "Lucas?"

Lucas blinked. Everyone else was looking at him. "Ah. Yes. My assignment is complete. The stalker made an attempt upon my client's life. I captured him and delivered him to the police."

"That's it?" Destiny leaned over and punched his arm. "Give us the details! That's where the fun is."

She grinned at him, her warm brown eyes crinkling at the corners. To make herself look younger, she'd put her hair in tiny braids that fell across her merry face. Unlike some of the others, Destiny had accepted him from the beginning, inviting him to get-togethers and treating him as if he was no different from anyone else. At first he hadn't liked that—after all, he *was* a prince and a dragon, and was not like everyone else—but he'd come to appreciate her open-hearted nature.

Lucas looked around the room, observing all the people he'd probably never see again—all the people he'd been putting off informing that he'd never see again. Fiona, the snow leopard, whose cool reserve was almost fit for royalty. Rafa, who had soon joined with Destiny in dragging Lucas to strange places like sports bars and barbecue joints, trying in his own way to make him feel like he belonged.

Shane, who had done his terrifying best to intimidate Lucas, but who had respected him when Lucas had passed his test of courage.

3

Nick, the former gangster, whose rough street background made him dislike people born into wealth, but who had backed Lucas up like a brother when they'd worked together.

Hal, who had invited him to join the team in the first place. Ellie, Hal's sweet and brave mate. Now that Ellie had finished doctoring Hal to her satisfaction, she leaned so close into him that she was practically sitting in his lap, her head against his shoulder and his arm around her back. That was the mate bond: comfort and companionship, passion and love.

A pang of loneliness pierced Lucas to the heart. He'd run out of time, and now he'd never experience that bond. And he couldn't bring himself to tell his teammates he'd have to leave forever—not when there was still a chance of a miracle.

He remembered a story his old nanny Vasilica had told him. Once there was a horse trainer who had been sentenced to death by the king.

"Wait!" the horse trainer had cried. "If you postpone my execution for one year, I can teach your horse to fly."

The king (who must have been very gullible, Lucas had always thought) had agreed to postpone the execution, but told the horse trainer that if he failed to teach his horse to fly by the end of it, he'd not only be executed, he'd be tortured to death.

The horse trainer's best friend approached him afterward and said, "What was the point of that bargain? You only bought yourself a year, and then you'll be tortured to death!"

The horse trainer replied, "Many things can happen in a year. In a year, I could die, or the horse could die, or the king could die. And who knows? In a year, maybe I really can teach a horse to fly!"

"Lucas?" Hal asked, frowning. "Are you all right? Did something happen that you're not telling us?"

Lucas glanced at the clock. Twelve hours. Maybe in twelve hours, he'd die, or the princess would die, or Brandusa would be invaded and no one would care about the arrangement. Or maybe in twelve hours, he'd find his mate.

"Nothing of note," Lucas replied, and recounted his latest job in more detail. He had been trained from childhood to speak in public, and he let his training take over.

After the meeting, the group had lunch. Lucas didn't notice what

he was eating, intent only on finishing so he could leave and go...
somewhere his mate might be.

Ellie stepped aside to text on her phone. Lucas watched her absent-
ly, wondering if she was talking to her brother Ethan, a Recon Marine
who was off on another mission. Then he decided from her giggles that
she was chatting with her best friend, Catalina Mendez, a paramedic
like herself. No one in Protection, Inc. had ever met her. Catalina, who
was even more adventurous than Ellie, volunteered with Paramedics
Without Borders. Soon after Ellie had met Hal, Catalina had been
called away to help with an earthquake in another country.

Could *she* be his mate?

"Ellie?" Lucas called. "When is Catalina coming back?"

Ellie's eyebrows rose; Lucas had never been curious about Catalina
before. "Hard to say. Whenever the emergency services in Loredana get
back on their feet."

That caught Lucas's attention. "Is that where she is? That's near my
country, Brandusa."

Everyone stared at him. Again.

"Didn't you know about the earthquake in Loredana?" Fiona inquired. "If it's near your country..."

Her words stung Lucas far more than she'd probably intended. He
detested the implication that he was neglecting his duties to the land
he'd left. He straightened his back and inquired, "Why should I pay
special attention to a region to which I will never return?"

His tone would have made most people back off, but Ellie didn't
scare easily. She asked, "Why'd you leave?"

Lucas said stiffly, "I had my reasons."

Destiny slapped Ellie's shoulder. "Don't bother. We've all asked,
but he won't say. Even Hal doesn't know."

Lucas felt an arrogant expression form on his face, like a mask. He
was no more than a couple meters from the farthest of them, but he felt
a million kilometers away. And he felt even more distant when he realized that after all this time, he still thought in meters and kilometers
instead of American feet and miles.

He'd fled Brandusa partly to escape the feeling that he was always
alone, even in company. But nothing had changed. He was still in
company, and he was still alone.

5

Everyone was *still* looking at him. Ellie seemed puzzled, Rafa and Destiny frowned in exasperation, Nick's glare was outright angry, and Fiona and Shane had applied their best "too cool to care" expressions. Lucas could deal with all that. But Hal looked concerned, and that was the one thing Lucas couldn't face.

"Lucas—" Hal began.

Lucas pushed back his chair and stood up. "I have work to do."

He walked out, the door swinging gently shut behind him. Slamming it would be beneath his dignity.

Lucas paused in the lobby to look at the framed photos of everyone's shift forms. Rafa's lion, lazing with his family. Hal's huge grizzly bear, at home in the forest. Fiona's snow leopard, lithe and deadly. Nick's fierce wolf, at the head of his pack. Destiny's tiger, stalking through the jungle. Shane's panther, whose yellow eyes seemed to burn through the photo. And Lucas's dragon, soaring over a castle in Brandusa. Another pang of loneliness pierced him at the thought of Hal taking down his picture.

He had to get control of himself. These feelings were also beneath him. He was a prince and a dragon. He had honor and dignity. And that was all that mattered.

Lucas got his car and drove aimlessly along the streets of Santa Martina. He watched all the passing women walking down the sidewalk, driving their cars, shopping and chatting and working. Out of all the billions of people in the world, one was his mate. But what were the odds that he would ever meet her?

Maybe she *was* Catalina.

Maybe she was a woman in a country he'd never even heard of, whose language he didn't speak.

Maybe she was right here in Santa Martina, but had never happened to be in the same place as him. Ellie and Hal had lived in Santa Martina for years before they'd met.

Maybe she was dead.

Maybe she hadn't yet been born.

Maybe she wouldn't be born until after he was dead.

Lucas drove until the setting sun turned the clouds to puffs of flame. Then, resigned, he headed for his apartment. As he walked upstairs, he thought, *Maybe Raluca found her mate.*

And maybe in a year, I can teach a horse to fly.

By the time he reached the landing, he wasn't surprised to see the tall, straight-backed, gray-haired figure, one arm rising to knock on Lucas's door. Lucas didn't need to see his face to know him.

"Grand Duke Vaclav," Lucas called.

His great-uncle turned around. He had tutored Lucas in etiquette, politics, logic, rhetoric, and swordfighting since he'd been a little boy, often remarking that praise made children soft and a prince needed to be strong. He was a man of his word; Lucas only knew he'd done something perfectly when his great-uncle nodded silently rather than finding something to critique.

The Grand Duke's stern expression didn't soften as he said, "Prince Lucas. I have come to summon you home to marry Princess Raluca."

Lucas's heart sank into his shoes. Though he knew it was a foolish, obvious thing to say, he couldn't help asking, "So she hasn't found her mate?"

His great-uncle's disapproving stare made Lucas feel like he was ten years old again. "Have you forgotten your lessons in logic after a mere five years? The terms of the treaty stated that if either you or Princess Raluca found your mate, the marriage would not take place. Given that I have come to summon you to marry her, is it possible that she has found her mate?"

"No," Lucas started to mutter, then remembered that he wasn't ten. He was twenty-three. He was an adult who had been living by himself for five years. He had protected others with his life. He might have to return to his childhood home, but he didn't have to return to his childhood.

Lucas forced himself to meet his great-uncle's cold black eyes. "I was not engaging in a debate, Grand Duke Vaclav. I was making conversation. Have you forgotten your own lessons in rhetoric? That was a rhetorical question."

Lucas had the small satisfaction of seeing his great-uncle look abashed, though it only lasted for a second.

"Indeed. Well, enough conversation. It is time for you to leave this... place... and do your duty." Grand Duke Vaclav made *place* sound like *hovel*. His disapproving gaze drew Lucas's attention to every way in which his apartment was not a palace.

Lucas couldn't help bristling. "May I invite you into my *place* for refreshment before you depart?"

His great-uncle folded his arms. "No. I will wait here while you set your affairs in order. We are expected at the castle tomorrow night."

That gave Lucas a couple hours, at most, to dispose of his apartment, his possessions, and his job.

His entire life.

Lucas looked at Grand Duke Vaclav—looked *down* at him. With a shock, he realized that he was now taller than his great-uncle.

Grand Duke Vaclav had no true power over him. He couldn't physically drag Lucas back to Brandusa. Nor was any arranged marriage agreement legally binding in America. All Lucas had to do to make the whole thing go away was to refuse to cooperate. His great-uncle would have to fly back to Brandusa empty-handed. Lucas and Raluca would be free to keep searching for their mates, and perhaps someday find them. Lucas could keep working at Protection, Inc.

As if his great-uncle had read his thoughts, he said, "You swore an oath, Prince Lucas. On your honor and by your hoard. If neither you nor Princess Raluca found your mate in five years, then you must marry each other."

Lucas replied icily, "Do you question my honor or my memory?"

"Neither." Grand Duke Vaclav's voice stayed cool, but Lucas felt the knife twist as he went on, "It was a rhetorical statement."

Lucas unlocked his door without another word. He barely stopped himself from slamming it behind him. Once the door closed, he found himself shaking with anger he was honor-bound to suppress.

And that would be his life from now on.

He looked around his apartment. It was sparely but elegantly furnished, unlike the lavish opulence of the palace. He had enjoyed creating a home just for himself, to please no one but himself. Now everything he did would be a joint decision with Raluca, plus consultation with his family and perhaps some important courtiers and members of parliament.

But there was nothing to be done. He hadn't taught the horse to fly, and now he had to ride it.

Without giving himself time to think, Lucas picked up the phone and called Hal.

"Ready to tell me what's going on?" Hal asked, without even saying hello first.

"I am. There is something I have never told you. When I was eighteen, I was promised in marriage. It is part of a treaty between my country, Brandusa, and a neighboring country, Viorel." Lucas summarized the story of his arranged marriage to Princess Raluca of Viorel and the oath they both had sworn. "That is why I left Brandusa, Hal. I did not wish to marry the princess, and I hoped to find my mate elsewhere. But I never found her, and so I must go."

"But—" Hal sounded more at a loss than Lucas had ever heard before. "Lucas, have you even met this princess? What if she *is* your mate, after all?"

"We have met. We are not mates. That is why we were allowed to wait for five years. Every dragon must be permitted a chance to seek out their mate."

"What happens if you get married, and then one of you finds your mate?"

"Honor takes precedence. Dragons do not divorce."

"Then don't marry her!" Hal's deep voice almost made the phone vibrate in Lucas's hand. "Tell them all to go to hell. You'll be doing the princess a favor, too."

Lucas's jaw was clenched so tightly, his teeth hurt. He forced his mouth open. "You do not understand. It is a matter of honor. Without honor, I have nothing—I *am* nothing."

"I don't see the honor in marrying someone you don't love and who doesn't love you!" Hal spoke in a growl; his bear was close to the surface.

Lucas's anger and bitterness chilled into an icy numbness. Of course Hal didn't understand. No American could understand. What did it matter that Lucas had to leave this country, where he had never fit in anyway—could never fit in?

"Hal, I leave you my car, my apartment, and everything in it. Keep them or give them away or sell them, as you please." Lucas hesitated, remembering how Destiny loved riding in his Porsche Carrera. "No. I leave you my apartment and possessions. Please give Destiny my car."

"This is crazy, Lucas!" Hal shouted so loudly, Lucas was forced to hold the phone away from his ear. "You sit tight. I'm rounding up whoever's available, and we're coming to your apartment to talk some sense into you."

Lucas spoke quickly; Hal did not live far away. "Ah, and also on second thought, give Rafa my apartment. He jokes about getting a 'swinging bachelor pad,' but perhaps he would truly enjoy one."

"I'm not giving anyone anything of yours, because you're not leaving!" Hal yelled.

"Let the others look through my possessions. If they see anything they want, please let them take it." Lucas hated to give up his favorite weapon, a gold-plated custom pistol, but guns were illegal in Brandusa. With a sigh, he said, "Shane may have my Desert Eagle. He will treat it with the care it deserves."

Hal spoke with quiet urgency. "Lucas, don't go anywhere. I'll be right there."

"The key will be under the mat."

The line clicked as Hal hung up. Lucas hoped Hal had heard him.

Unlike most shifters, dragons could take their clothing and some additional weight with them when they transformed. Lucas had always supposed it was from necessity. If dragons had to leave behind their gold when they shifted, they would probably never shift at all.

He opened the safe that contained his hoard. His dragon's lust for gold and jewels took him even in his haste, and for several seconds he stood mesmerized by the exquisite glitter of his treasure. Then he poured the precious gems and gold coins into a pouch and tied it around his waist, and put on all the jewelry. The chill and weight of gold was soothing on his skin.

Lucas caught sight of himself as he strode past a reflective window, with jeweled rings on every finger and heavy gold chains wrapped around his throat and wrists. He looked like a king about to ride out to his death in a battle he knew he could not win.

He stepped out into the corridor, locked the door, and slipped the key under the mat. "I'm ready."

For the first time in Lucas's life, Grand Duke Vaclav gave him an approving nod. "Now you look like a proper prince."

Lucas hurried him up the stairs, expecting at any minute to hear the loud tread of Hal's footsteps behind them. When they got to the roof, he made a quick but thorough scan of the area. No one was in sight, and no planes or helicopters flew overhead.

"Conceal yourself," Grand Duke Vaclav warned him. "You do not know who might be watching."

"I know," Lucas snapped, and was annoyed to hear his own voice. He sounded like the resentful teenager he had once been. He had to keep hold of his real self: Lucas the man, not Lucas the boy.

He could tell already that it would be hard.

Grand Duke Vaclav drew in a deep breath. The air around him sparkled black. Lucas's vision blurred, and he felt the desire to look elsewhere, accompanied by the certainty that what he was looking at was ordinary and unimportant. But he kept watching. As a dragon shifter, he still felt the effects of draconic concealment, but unlike humans or non-dragon shifters, he could resist them.

The black sparks became a whirlwind, then a blizzard. Grand Duke Vaclav vanished within the flurry. Then the sparks winked out of existence. Where a gray-haired man had once stood, a dragon crouched. Every scale and claw gleamed black as if it had been carved from polished iron.

"Lucas!"

He spun around. Hal and Nick burst through the stairs and stood facing him. Hal must have found Nick in the gym; his chest was bare, and his black hair and werewolf gang tattoos glistened with sweat.

"I am sorry, Hal. I…" Lucas swallowed against a lump in his throat. "I have very much enjoyed working at Protection, Inc. I shall never forget it."

"What the hell are you talking about?" Nick burst out. "And what's with all that bling?"

The iron dragon's obsidian eyes narrowed in contempt. He launched off the roof and rose into the sky, then dipped a wingtip, urging Lucas to join him.

Hal and Nick couldn't see the dragon, but Hal must have spotted Lucas's gaze shift.

"Is someone here with you?" Hal asked. His hand was on his gun; so was Nick's. "Lucas, are you leaving of your own free will?"

No, Lucas thought. *I am leaving because honor compels me.*

But Hal wouldn't understand that.

"No one can force a dragon to do anything." Lucas lowered his

11

gaze, unable to meet the frustrated concern in Hal's hazel eyes or the hot anger in Nick's green eyes. "Farewell."

He reached within himself, seeking his dragon. Lucas drew upon his lust for gold, his joy in flight, and the assured power and detachment that he could only imitate as a human. He saw Hal and Nick begin to run forward. Then he was lost in his own transformation, his blood burning through his veins like molten gold, his body expanding like a butterfly breaking free of its cocoon.

His wings stretched out, his powerful legs tensed, and then he was aloft, soaring above the rooftop. The two humans shrank below, frustration and anger in every line of their bodies. Their faces turned upward, seeking him, but whether they could see him or not, he was out of their reach.

The part of Lucas that belonged to the man felt his heart crack into a million tiny pieces. Then his dragon took over. He twisted easily in the air, his wings stroking upward, shedding all feelings but glory in the freedom of the sky.

The gold dragon followed the iron dragon, heading home.

Lucas preferred to fly at a leisurely pace and watch the land below. But his great-uncle urged him onward, faster and faster, casting disdainful glances whenever Lucas lagged.

Lucas's sigh came out in a puff of flame. Despite his resolve, he had no desire to arrive sooner. But he beat his powerful wings until he passed the iron dragon. He maintained that position for the rest of the trip, a full night and day in the air. They landed only briefly, to drink from lakes and to hunt a pair of deer for their supper. Lucas was just as happy to stay a dragon for the trip. He did not enjoy conversing with his great-uncle.

When he was aloft, Lucas focused on flight and tried not to think of anything else. He especially tried not to think of how he'd fled from his own teammates without preparing them for his departure because of his foolish hope that he wouldn't have to leave and his cowardice in wishing not to explain it to their faces.

He might be leaving to fulfill a vow of honor, but the way he'd left had been anything but honorable. Even if a miracle occurred and his mate ran to greet him when he landed, he'd never be able to face anyone in Protection, Inc. again.

Land and sea flashed by beneath his wings. As the sun began to set, Lucas saw the familiar dense forests and peaked roofs of Brandusa. He slowed, spiraling downward, until the turrets and towers of his ancestral palace came into view. The soft glow of its golden marble and the sparkle of its inlay of real gold gave him a pang of mixed resentment and nostalgia.

He braked his speed as he descended to the walled courtyard and the mossy floor, which was tended constantly by gardeners to provide a comfortable landing surface. Then his talons touched down.

Lucas was home.

A crowd of courtiers, servants, and family hurried to greet him and Grand Duke Vaclav, who had landed behind him. The dragon shifters must have spotted them flying in. Lucas became a man and drew himself up, his great-uncle's lessons in deportment echoing in his ears: *spine straight, shoulders back, chest out, chin up.*

He greeted everyone as was proper for their station, from a polite nod to the servant who offered him a damp cloth to wipe his face to a formal embrace of his aunt and uncle, Queen Livia and King Andrei. His own mixed emotions at his return were mirrored in their faces: though they had always been kind to him, he was sure they'd have preferred him to find his mate in America and never return.

The throne of Brandusa had passed to them after his parents died when he was ten, as he had been far too young to rule. But he remained crown prince and would become king upon their deaths. Their own children could only inherit the crown if Lucas renounced it or died without having children himself.

Lucas glanced into the crowd. Sure enough, his cousins' faces displayed thin veils of welcome over their actual feelings of dislike and resentment.

He sighed. If it wasn't for honor, he'd have been thrilled to hand over his position to them and let them all duel each other for the crown when the time came.

Queen Livia gave him a slightly wistful but genuine smile. "How lovely to see you again, Lucas."

King Andrei shook his hand hard. "Yes, indeed. Welcome home!"

The king and queen had aged more than Lucas had expected. They were only middle-aged, but their faces were lined and silver strands glittered in their black hair. Even in the partly-ceremonial position that royalty now held in Brandusa, ruling a country was obviously not easy. And though they were quite fond of each other, they were not mates, but had participated in an arranged marriage meant to strengthen ties between their countries. For the first time, Lucas wondered if either of them had ever met their mate after they were married and it was too late.

After a long exchange of greetings and catching-up, Queen Livia said, "You must be weary, Lucas. I have arranged for you and Princess Raluca to have a quiet dinner for two. Then you must get some rest. Your engagement ball is tomorrow night."

"What?" Lucas exclaimed. He felt like the ground had been yanked out from under his feet. Again. "I thought those things took months to prepare!"

"They do," Queen Livia replied calmly. "We have been preparing it for months. All we need from you is your attendance."

Lucas couldn't help turning to his great-uncle, feeling unreasonably betrayed. "You could have told me."

"It was my honor to escort you back to the palace, your highness," Grand Duke Vaclav said, not sounding apologetic in the slightest. Then he bowed and departed.

King Andrei cleared his throat. "Lucas, Princess Raluca's uncle, Duke Constantine, has graced us with his presence."

Lucas, who had been pretending not to see him, gave the duke a formal bow. "How kind of you to join us."

Duke Constantine smirked. "Oh, the pleasure was all mine."

Lucas supposed it was unfair to dislike the duke, given that they barely knew each other. But Duke Constantine stood to profit immensely by the trade treaty that would be signed when the marriage occurred. Lucas had always suspected that he favored the marriage because it benefited himself, not his country. Now, seeing how the duke openly gloated, Lucas was certain of it.

Gritting his teeth, Lucas turned away from the duke to greet the servants. It was a small slight, but he couldn't resist it.

Lucas's old nanny, Vasilica, inspected him from head to toe, clucking in disapproval. "Such strange clothes you're wearing! Your highness, you must be measured by the tailors before you sleep tonight. The attire prepared for the ball was made from your last measurements. It will not do."

His cousin Adelina shot him a look of equal disapproval, but expressed it with a dainty sniff. "Indeed. You are much larger now, Lucas. I had heard that Americans are all enormous from stuffing themselves with *burgers* and *fries*—" She spoke the words as if she'd said *slugs* and *roaches*. "—but I expected you to have more self-control."

It was true that Lucas had gained weight since he was eighteen, but it was muscle, not fat. Annoyed, he shot back, "Your own self-control is formidable, Adelina. I am impressed at your efforts to reduce yourself to a skeleton."

"Children!" Vasilica scolded, as if they were both ten. "Come along, Lucas. The princess is waiting."

Lucas followed her into the palace, glad to escape his catty cousin and the nosy crowd of courtiers. He felt dazed. How could the ball be *tomorrow?* He'd thought he'd have months to prepare himself. Instead, he'd have a night and a day.

His footsteps echoed on the marble floors. Everyone who saw him stopped to bow and greet him, so his progress was slow. Seeing more people brought home to him how poorly he fit in. He still wore the tailored suit he'd had on at Protection, Inc. It was perfectly cut and expensive, but formal dress in Brandusa consisted of colorful tunics and breeches. He stood out like a crow in a flock of parrots.

And he couldn't even change for dinner, because Vasilica was right—his old clothes wouldn't fit him now. Like many dragons, he had been slow to reach his full adult growth. He was six inches taller and forty pounds heavier than when he'd been eighteen.

Vasilica stopped before the most lavish guest chamber in the palace. Lucas knew it well. Princess Raluca had stayed in it the last time they had met, when they had both been eighteen.

His old nurse winked at him, making her many wrinkles deepen. "Go on, your highness!"

She bustled away, leaving Lucas alone in front of the door. It was hundreds of years old, carved with flying dragons. Five years ago, Raluca had closed it in his face after telling him that she would pray nightly that he found his mate, for she could never love him.

You are a prince and a dragon, he reminded himself. *Do not add to the cowardice you have already committed this day.*

He knocked on the door. "Hello? It's Lucas."

Raluca opened it. "Come in."

He walked into the chamber. The door closed behind him with a final-sounding click.

The last time he had seen her, she had been taller than him and painfully self-conscious about it, with bones too pronounced for her skinny frame. Her hair had been the color of ash, and her skin and lips so pale that she forever appeared on the verge of fainting. Only her eyes had been beautiful, gray as storm clouds and framed with thick black lashes.

Raluca had changed. She had grown into her height and seemed comfortable with it, radiating graceful poise. Her chiseled bones now lent her a fierce and elegant beauty. Her skin was flawless ivory, her lips were red as wine, and her hair shone silver as molten metal. Not a trace remained of the awkward girl she'd been, except for her storm-gray eyes.

His fiancée-to-be was every inch the dragon princess now. She was beautiful. Exquisite. A treasure any dragon would be proud to claim.

And yet she was nothing more to him than a lovely stranger.

Raluca too was looking him over. Unexpectedly, she let out a chiming laugh, then clapped a slim hand to her mouth. "I'm sorry. I am not laughing *at* you. Only at my memory of how awkward we both were. I am glad I am no longer eighteen."

"So am I." Spotting the table set for two, he formally bowed and offered Raluca his arm. "Shall we dine?"

She took his arm, allowing him to escort her to the table. Lucas tried to ignore the pointed selection of food—champagne, oysters on the half-shell, roast venison in berry sauce, and broiled quails—all of which was considered either romantic or aphrodisiac.

He'd dated in the years since he'd left Brandusa. He'd even had affairs with women. None had made him catch fire inside, as mates were said to do, but he had enjoyed himself. This would be no different.

Raluca was a charming dinner companion, not to mention extraordinarily beautiful. The dinner passed pleasantly enough until Lucas reached for the dessert, a golden globe set into a platter filled with ice. When he uncovered it, he was confronted by a heart-shaped raspberry sorbet decorated with a scattering of red rose petals and a pair of chocolate wedding rings covered in edible gold foil.

Lucas and Raluca stared at the romantic dessert, then at each other. The acute embarrassment he felt was mirrored on her face. Then they both burst out laughing. Lucas supposed it was either laugh, or fling themselves out the window and refrain from shifting on the way down.

"I hope it's as delicious as it is unsubtle," Raluca said at last.

Lucas removed the rings, then took the gold spoons and molded the heart into a diamond. "There! Now it's a reference to a game of cards."

Raluca snapped the wedding rings into small pieces and scattered them atop the diamond. "And the coins one might win."

He smiled at her, the chill in his heart easing a little. "Do you wish this marriage, Raluca? If you choose to refuse it, I will too. I would not let you accept dishonor alone."

Her chin lifted and she straightened her back. Someone had taught her just as Grand Duke Vaclav had taught him. Her uncle, Duke Constantine, perhaps. "I swore a vow of honor on my country and on my hoard. Many dragons before us have had such marriages. It is only the lucky few who find their mates."

Lucas stifled a sigh, realizing how much he'd hoped she would beg him to break his vow. "That is true."

"But it was kind of you to offer." She smiled, though a shadow of sadness clouded her gray eyes, and took his hands in hers. "Let us make the best of this partnership. It need not be terrible. We clearly have much in common. I hope we may become great friends."

"I believe that we shall." Lucas squeezed her delicate hands, wishing that everything could be different. He sincerely liked her. He would do his best to be a good husband to her.

They ate the dessert, but Lucas didn't taste it any more than he'd tasted the rest of the meal. It was impossible to forget that at midnight tomorrow, he would be engaged to a woman who could never truly love him and whom he could never love as she deserved.

Tick-tock.

CHAPTER TWO
Journey

Journey Jacobson always imagined herself as Cinderella when she hauled out the ashes. As she dumped the ash bucket out on the compost heap, a flock of colorful wild parakeets flew up from a nearby tree and circled above her head, making annoyed-sounding chirps.

Journey was pretty sure that had happened in *Cinderella*, too. But since she couldn't afford either an internet connection or an international call, she couldn't check. Instead, she stood and watched the parakeets flutter against the sapphire sky. When she'd first come to Brandusa, she'd been amazed at the flocks of wild parakeets with their feathers of pastel green, blue, pink, lavender, or yellow. They were like living Easter decorations. She'd been in Brandusa for three months now, and they still amazed her.

The parakeets settled back down into their tree. With a sigh, Journey hefted her bucket. She'd have been happy to stay in Brandusa longer, but she was about to lose her position with the Florescu family, who paid her a small salary plus room and board to be an au pair and a companion for their seventeen-year-old daughter, Stefania. But Stefania was about to turn eighteen and no longer needed a chaperone.

The Florescus, who had grown fond of Journey, had helped her search for a new job. But to her dismay, she hadn't been able to find another position in the city. She had enough money saved for a plane ticket out of the country, but none left over to cover her expenses while she searched for a new job. It looked like her year of backpacking across

Europe was over.

"Oh, well," she said to the parakeets. She'd spent so much time in cities where no one spoke English that she'd gotten in the habit of talking to animals. They couldn't talk back either, but at least they didn't give her annoyed or embarrassed or apologetic glances when she addressed them in English. "It was wonderful while it lasted. I got to live my dream! And at least I'm going out with a bang."

The parakeets chirped excitedly, as if they wanted to hear more.

"I'm going to a ball at the palace!" Journey informed them. "Can you imagine? Stefania was invited, so I'm going as her chaperone. I don't have suitable clothes and I can't quite fit into hers, so her mother is going to help me dig through the attic to find something I can wear. The ball is traditional garb only, so it won't matter if it's old—it won't be out of fashion."

The parakeets seemed to approve of this plan. A bubblegum pink parakeet flapped its wings and a powder blue parakeet let out a piercing screech.

"I'll remember the ball for the rest of my life," Journey said. "It'll cheer me up while I'm flipping burgers or telemarketing or selling shoes or whatever I end up doing in America."

The thought of those jobs depressed her. Locked up in a room, probably in some dull suburb with rent she could afford, socking away every spare cent for years until she'd finally earned enough money to go backpacking again... Ugh!

Maybe she could get a job as a traveling salesperson. Or a taxi driver. Anything to stay on the move, even if it was only within a single town.

With a final wave and whistle to the parakeets, Journey hefted her ash bucket and went back inside the Florescu house. As always, she paused to admire the carved wooden door. It was a Brandusan tradition that she especially admired. Every household had a door carved with something associated with the family that lived in it. Even the poorest homes carved their own with whatever level of skill they could manage—which was always impressive to Journey's untutored eyes, for woodworking was a skill that every child learned.

The Florescu door was carved with twining roses. Every leaf and petal was intricately detailed, some complete with fuzzy bees or drops of dew. No matter how often Journey looked at it, she always found some new detail to enjoy. Today she spotted a tiny butterfly, wings folded and thread-thin proboscis extended, half-hidden by petals as it drank from a rose. She sighed with admiration.

"We will be very sorry to lose you, Journey," said Mrs. Florescu. The plump, middle-aged woman smiled as she walked up. "I've so enjoyed seeing how much you appreciate our culture. I wish I'd been able to find another family for you to work for."

"I know you tried. I really appreciate it."

"Normally, it wouldn't be hard. But right now everyone's worried about money. It's because of the new trade treaty with Viorel that will be sealed with Prince Lucas's engagement—many people think it will benefit Viorel at the expense of Brandusa. You see, the former tax agreement…" Mrs. Florescu broke off with a laugh. "Never mind. I shouldn't bore you with politics when you have a ball gown to find! Go wash up, then meet me in the attic."

Journey replaced the ash bucket by the fireplace and took a quick bath, then eagerly went up the winding stairs and into the attic. Mrs. Florescu was already there, opening carved trunks bound with brass and pulling out gowns and undergarments and shoes. She had set up a lovely full-length mirror for Journey to look at herself under the shaft of golden sun from the skylight.

Mrs. Florescu examined Journey's body, then nodded in satisfaction. "Very good! You have the body of a proper Brandusan girl. Big belly to withstand hard winters, wide hips to bear children easily, and good plump breasts to nurse babies and please your husband!"

Journey laughed, enjoying Mrs. Florescu's frankness. "I wish I was a Brandusan girl! The proper American body has slim hips to wriggle into designer jeans, a flat belly to look good in a bikini, and big fake breasts made out of silicone."

Mrs. Florescu made a face. "False breasts! Who thinks of such things? No, it will be easy to find clothing that will be lovely on your figure. It is only your hair that is unusual for Brandusa."

"It's unusual in the US, too." Journey looked in the mirror. The sunlight fell directly on her wild tumble of red curls, making them glow like flames.

"The royal family is the same way," Mrs. Florescu remarked, sorting through gowns. "Prince Lucas has golden hair, and his promised, Princess Raluca, has hair of silver. It is the mark of the dragon."

Journey smiled to herself. Out of everything in Brandusa, perhaps what she loved the best was the legend that the royal family did not merely have the dragon as their sigil, but could actually transform into dragons. When she had first arrived, she had thought that people who mentioned it were being metaphoric or poetic, but she had eventually realized that they sincerely believed it. Journey had traveled enough to know that every culture had their own beliefs that seemed strange to people from other cultures—Americans included. So she never argued or expressed disbelief. Besides, she loved the idea that the king and queen flew invisibly over the city every night, ensuring that all was well.

"Maybe someone will mistake me for a princess," Journey suggested, grinning. "I could be a ruby dragon!"

Mrs. Florescu shook her head, as if that was a perfectly reasonable possibility that merely happened to be incorrect. "Dragons are very slim. It is because flying requires so much energy."

Journey would have loved to coax her for more details on the royal dragons, but Mrs. Florescu held up a handful of undergarments instead. "Here, put these on."

Unselfconsciously, Journey stripped down to her panties, then let Mrs. Florescu help her into a corset. It wasn't uncomfortable—in fact, it provided good back support. It also lifted and supported her breasts, pushing them together to make her cleavage even more impressive than usual. Then she put on several layer of petticoats, clean and rustling and scented with dried roses, and after that a white undergown with a tight bodice and long embroidered sleeves.

Finally, Mrs. Florescu helped her into a long dress, then turned her around to look into the mirror. "There!"

The sleeveless gown was leaf-green, making her eyes and hair look even brighter and giving a flattering cast to her freckled skin. The full skirt ended at her ankles, sparing her the worry of being able to dance in it. The neckline was very low-cut, showing off her cleavage. It had crisscross green lacing down the front, allowing the white undergown bodice to show through.

But her favorite part was what made Brandusan traditional dress distinctive: the undergown sleeves. They were embroidered with crimson roses on green vines, as delicately detailed as the roses carved into the front door. The vines twined up her arms and over her shoulders, as if she was decked in living flowers.

"Thank you so much," Journey breathed. "You're so kind, Mrs. Florescu."

"I knew it would suit you," said Mrs. Florescu, seeming pleased with her own judgment. She picked up a pair of shoes, and said, "Shoes last. If you're not used to them, it will be difficult to climb stairs."

They walked down to Stefania's room and knocked on the door.

"Come!" Stefania called.

They went inside. Mrs. Florescu and Journey had already helped Stefania dress and do her hair and makeup, before Journey had finished her last chores. Stefania wasn't quite as curvy (and often remarked enviously on Journey's figure), but her crimson gown showed off the curves she did have. She too wore a white undergown embroidered with red roses. With her black hair braided and pinned atop her head, her pale skin, and her full scarlet lips, she reminded Journey of Snow White.

Stefania gave Journey a delighted smile. "Oh, you're so pretty! Perhaps you'll meet a rich Brandusan man, and then you can marry and never leave. And perhaps I will meet another!"

Mrs. Florescu gave her daughter a stern look before turning to Journey. "She is not to be alone with any man. She is still too young. You need not stick close together in the ballroom, but she is not to go into any side rooms without you."

"Oh, Ma," Stefania sighed. "I turn eighteen tomorrow!"

Ignoring her comment, her mother continued, "She may dance with any man, but she is not to choose one and keep him from dancing with other women. Even the prince will dance with many women, not only his fiancée-to-be."

Stefania's eyes lit up as she clasped Journey's hands. "Let's both try to dance with the prince! It's good luck to dance with the dragon."

Journey doubted that a prince would select a broke American backpacker out of the hundreds of beautiful women at the ball. But with any luck he'd be willing to give a sweet teenager a memory she'd always treasure. "I'll do my best to make sure *you* get to dance with him. I'm happy just to be there."

"Sit down," said Mrs. Florescu. "Stefania and I will do your hair and makeup."

Journey sat patiently while Stefania applied her makeup and Mrs. Florescu did her best to tame Journey's curly hair.

"You will be the wild rose," Mrs. Florescu said at last, giving up the attempt. "Now put on your dancing shoes."

Journey's shoes were made of polished brown wood and green leather, with a lining of red leather. The green leather was cut out in rose shapes, allowing the red to show through. Stefania's were of black wood and red leather, with leaf-shaped cutouts to a green leather lining.

Journey didn't often wear high heels, much less dance in them. But the heels weren't too high, more like swing dancing shoes than the teetering icepick heels supermodels wore.

"Mind you don't let Stefania run wild," Mrs. Florescu warned Journey.

"Oh, Ma," Stefania sighed again. "What do you think I'll do, run off with the prince?"

To Journey's surprise, Mrs. Florescu neither laughed nor frowned. Instead, she looked thoughtful. "Do you think I would object if you were his mate? Stefania—it is the last chance, for him and for you. Mind you look into his eyes!"

Journey had no idea what Mrs. Florescu was talking about. Maybe it was good luck to make eye contact with unmarried royalty.

"Yes, Ma." Stefania seized Journey's hands. "Let's go!"

They hurried out of the house and into the hired carriage that awaited them outside. That was something else Journey never got tired of: the horse-drawn carriages. Motor vehicles were banned within one mile of the palace, so carriages often shared the road with cars, bicycles, motorcycles, and the occasional rider on horseback.

Their carriage was drawn by a pair of lovely snow-white horses with pink ribbons braided into their manes. The coachman had a pointed nose and beady eyes that gave him an unfortunate resemblance to a rat, but he wore an elegant black uniform. He cracked his whip and away they went, clattering over the cobblestones.

The streets were decorated with gold and silver ornaments in honor of the prince's engagement. The setting sun made them glow like molten metal. Journey imagined the prince and princess flying overhead to observe the carriages jolting toward the palace.

The carriage pulled up at the palace gates, and Journey and Stefania got out. Journey had seen the palace and its gardens before, but she'd never gone inside the magnificent building of golden marble whose towers pierced the sky.

She thrilled with excitement as she walked through the immense double doors carved with dragons soaring, dragons fighting in midair, dragons hatching from eggs, dragons guarding treasure hoards, and dragons doing every possible other thing that dragons could do. She'd have loved to examine the doors more closely, but Stefania was practically exploding with impatience.

The ballroom took Journey's breath away. Its high ceilings sparkled with crystal-and-gold chandeliers, couples were dancing on the polished floors, and a full orchestra played on a stage. The Brandusan tunes were quick and merry, making Journey's heart feel light enough to float to the ceiling. Her time in the country was winding to a close, but she'd make the most of it.

"Let me dance, Journey," Stefania begged. "I won't run away with anyone, I swear!"

"Go find the prince," Journey suggested.

"He's not here yet, silly," Stefania replied. "He makes his grand entrance later."

"Then go have fun. And don't go off alone with any men."

"I promise!"

Stefania darted away, her wooden heels clicking, and made a beeline for a handsome young man in knee-high black boots, blue breeches, and a blue tunic embroidered with white constellations. A moment later, they were whirling together across the dance floor, kicking up their heels in a folk dance Journey had never learned.

Journey watched the dancers for a while, enjoying the sight and making sure Stefania wasn't doing anything but flitting from one man to the next like a crimson butterfly. Then she headed for the tables and bars around the edges of the ballroom.

The tables were full of platters of elegantly arranged appetizers and desserts, and the bartenders offered cocktails, wine, or hot coffee or tea. One platter held traditional Brandusan pastries: apricot crescents, apple dumplings, plum buns, cherry tartlets, marmalade rolls, and poppy seed triangles. Another displayed fancier desserts: chocolate cream squares, meringue kisses, marzipan tortes, and elaborate concoctions of whipped cream and pastry decorated with gold dust.

She was just reaching out for a slice of apple strudel when the orchestra finished their tune. The dancers halted as the trumpeters played a fanfare. Stefania froze like an image in a snapshot, still clasping the hands of her latest dance partner. Everyone turned toward a platform at one end of the ballroom. As the fanfare ended, total silence fell.

Journey could feel the anticipation in the air. She too was caught up in it, eagerly awaiting her first sight of the prince and princess.

The personalities, hobbies, and adventures of the royal family were often the subject of gossip in Brandusa, so she knew all about the king and queen and their children. But she knew little about the royal family of Viorel, except that they were also supposed to be dragons. And, she realized, she knew barely anything about Prince Lucas, even though he was heir to the throne, other than that he had golden hair and had been abroad for years. But no one had ever mentioned what he was doing abroad or what he was like as a person. Journey hadn't noticed that before, but now the omission struck her as odd.

Before she had time to wonder about it, a man and a woman stepped on to the platform. Everyone bowed. Hastily, Journey did as well. Then she straightened. She was relatively close to the platform, so she got a good look at the prince and princess.

Princess Raluca was slim and lovely, young but with silver hair. She wore a Brandusan gown, red as blood. The undergown had black sleeves embroidered with silver dragons. She wore a delicate tiara of gold filigree studded with diamonds, and a matching necklace, bracelets, and rings.

Prince Lucas was tall and lean, with broad shoulders filling out his sky-blue tunic embroidered with golden dragons. His features were sharp but handsome, as if they had been chiseled from marble. His hair was as bright as sunlight, and his eyes were the color of amber. He wore a heavy gold chain around his throat, more gold chains wrapped around his wrists, and gold and diamond rings that flashed and sparkled in the light. He had beautiful hands, long-fingered and slim, but strong rather than delicate. They were the hands of a concert pianist, or a sculptor, or a swordfighter.

Guns were banned in Brandusa. The police carried batons and

26

criminals carried knives, and swordfighting was the national martial art. Between Prince Lucas's hands and the athletic grace with which he carried himself, Journey bet he was an excellent swordfighter.

Journey couldn't stop looking at Prince Lucas, drinking in every detail and searching for more. First she thought it was because he was royalty. Then she thought it was because he was so stunningly gorgeous, with his extraordinary amber eyes and golden hair. Then she realized that it was because he seemed so sad.

Why would he be sad? Journey thought. *He's the crown prince. He's gorgeous. He's rich. He's powerful. He's about to marry an incredibly beautiful woman. What has he got to be sad about?*

She didn't even know why she thought he was sad. He didn't *look* sad. He was smiling at the crowd. But there was something about him, maybe some tension in his shoulders or tightness around his mouth, which gave her that impression.

It made no sense, but she wanted to comfort him. She wanted to jump on to the platform, grab his hand and feel those strong fingers hold hers tight, and whisper, "Lucas, let's get out of here! Ditch that princess and run away with me!"

And then she'd see his eyes light up and the sorrow fall away from him, and he'd sweep her into his arms and run away with her. And then he'd take her to some other castle that he just happened to have (well, he *was* a prince), and tell her he'd fallen in love with her at first sight, and then he'd lay her down on a huge luxurious bed, and make wild and sweet love to her. All night.

Journey shook her head in amusement at her own wild imagination. But she had to admit, she'd enjoyed her silly little daydream. It had made her warm around the heart and hot in some other places, making her realize that she'd been cold for years. She liked to look at guys, sure, but it had been a long time since she'd felt more than a little tingle of turn-on. But a single glance at Prince Lucas had practically made her catch fire inside.

"Welcome, people of Brandusa!" Prince Lucas called out. His voice easily carried across the room; he'd obviously had vocal training. Journey liked the sound of it. He hadn't lost his accent in his five years abroad. She liked that, too. The Brandusan accent ranked with Irish for sexiness.

"Thank you, people of Brandusa, for welcoming me into your home," said Princess Raluca. Her voice chimed like crystal, exactly like one might imagine of a princess.

"Please, enjoy the food and drink and dancing," Prince Lucas went on. "Princess Raluca and I will mingle with you. We regret that we cannot dance and speak and drink with each one of you, but we shall do our best. We thank you for coming to celebrate our engagement and to witness the exchange of rings and vows at midnight. And now—"

Prince Lucas had been scanning the room, his gaze resting first on this person, then on that. As he said the word "now," his eyes met Journey's.

His polished speech broke off abruptly. His jaw dropped. And his amber eyes met hers with a force that made her jump. They seemed to brighten until they shone like molten gold. Prince Lucas stared at her with an intensity she couldn't help reading as passion, as if he *did* want to grab her and carry her away. As if love at first sight was real, and he'd just fallen in love with her.

Then he broke off eye contact. Looking fixedly away from her, he went on smoothly, "—enjoy the ball!"

Journey fell back to reality with a thud. As if a Brandusan prince would ever fall for an American backpacker! And any man who'd ditch his fiancée for a stranger was a total jerk—Prince Cheater, not Prince Charming.

She'd fallen for Prince Charming Asshole once before. And if there was one vow she'd hold herself to, it was to never make that mistake again.

CHAPTER THREE
Lucas

Lucas had been taught that dragons always knew their mates at first sight. When he'd asked, "But *how* do you know?" he'd always gotten the unhelpful reply, "You just do." He'd imagined it as simple recognition, like the difference between seeing a stranger and seeing someone you know.

Oh, he'd imagined thinking. *Oh, I know that person. That woman's my mate.*

Then, standing on the platform at his own engagement ball, he saw her.

Mine, his dragon hissed.

Every drop of blood in Lucas's veins was replaced with liquid fire. He burned with passion, with desire, with a wild and desperate longing.

It *was* a feeling of recognition, but not like spotting a friend from across the room. It was the kind of recognition that altered your entire being, the kind that made you know in an instant that your life would never be the same, the kind that made you realize what you'd been missing all your days before.

It was like becoming a dragon for the very first time. He had wings. He could fly. He could breathe fire. It was at once revelatory and completely natural. How could he have lived all those years without ever tasting the freedom of the skies? From the first instant of his first flight, even though he'd lived thirteen years without ever flying before, he knew down to his bones that if the power to shift was ever taken from him, he would die of longing for the open sky.

Lucas saw the woman in the gown of twining roses, with her emerald eyes and ruby hair, and knew she was the only one for him. If she would be his mate, he would love and cherish and protect her, treasuring her above his hoard and above his life. If he lost her, his heart would shatter like glass.

And he didn't even know her name.

He stood gaping like a fool, his speech forgotten. He could do nothing but stare at her delectable curves, her hair like embers, her sparkling eyes. Who was she? She didn't look Brandusan, and surely she was too young to be a diplomat. A diplomat's daughter?

A discreet cough from Raluca brought him back to his senses. He finished his speech on autopilot, then stepped down from the platform. Luckily, it was the custom to mingle with the crowd, so he didn't have to make a special excuse to talk to his mate. He strode through the crowd, smiling and bowing and exchanging greetings and good-wishes, his heart as light as if borne aloft on dragon wings.

Then he stood before her. The crowd faded away. All he could see was her. She was even more beautiful up-close, with a charming spray of freckles across her nose and cheeks. Her luscious breasts swelled up from her corset like living pearls. He took a deep breath, and caught a hint of her scent: dried roses and clean linen, and something warm and womanly beneath it. It made his head swim.

So this was his mate. He wanted to learn everything about her. He wanted to catch her up in his arms and feel the softness of her rosy lips.

He couldn't believe how lucky he'd been to have found her.

And he had no idea what to say.

"Welcome," he finally managed. "I am Lucas."

"I know," she said with a smile. Her accent was unmistakably American. She gave him a surprisingly graceful curtsy; she must have spent some time in Brandusa. "I'm Journey Jacobson."

"What a marvelous name. Did your parents give it to you or did you choose it for yourself?"

She cocked her head, sending her glinting curls tumbling over her shoulders. "You know, I always expect people to ask that, but they hardly ever do. Jacobson is my family name, but I chose Journey myself."

"How did you come to choose it?"

"I grew up in a little town called Lummox, North Dakota. There was basically nothing there but canola fields and cows."

"Canola?"

"It's a plant," Journey explained. "You squeeze oil out of the seed pods. It has yellow flowers and it's pretty in the spring, but there's only so long you can look at fields of yellow flowers. And that's about all there is to do in Lummox: look at the canola, and tip cows."

"Tip cows?" Lucas repeated, fascinated.

"They sleep standing up. If you push them hard, they fall over. Then they jump up and charge you, and you have to run. It's kind of mean. I never did it myself. But if your only alternative is watching the canola…"

Lucas couldn't help laughing. "I can see why you wished to journey."

She laughed with him. Her laughter wasn't like Raluca's, like crystal bells; it was full-throated and unselfconscious, and made him want to laugh too. "Oh, and also we had a library. A very tiny, dusty library, that no one ever went in but me and the librarian. It had three shelves full of ancient *National Geographics*. I read them over and over, and I decided that as soon as I was old enough, I'd get out of Lummox and see the world. But the thing was, a lot of people had dreams in Lummox. *Had*. Mostly, they'd given them up. So I decided to name myself for my dream, so I'd never forget it."

Journey had begun her story in laughter, but when she got to the part about people giving up their dreams, he saw her eyes glisten with held-back tears. Who had she known who'd given up their dreams? Her parents, perhaps?

Lucas didn't want to press her. How cruel he would be, to make her cry at a ball! Instead, he spoke the other thought that was in his heart. "How brave and clever of you to take your dream as your name. How old were you?"

"Thirteen." She smiled, her sorrow fading. "Everyone thought I was crazy. You don't change your first name in Lummox, North Dakota. You especially don't change it to something that isn't even a real name. I caught hell for it for the next five years. It took me an entire year to even get people to stop calling me Ashley."

"How did you manage it?"

She shrugged. "I answered when they called me Journey, and I didn't answer when they called me Ashley. For about six months, no one called me anything at all. Then they gave in."

"You have a will of steel."

That same sad look shadowed her face. "Maybe I did then."

Lucas was puzzled. "Always, surely. You succeeded, did you not? Here you are, journeying far from... Lummox."

Journey's sorrow melted into amusement. "I love the way you say it. It's like you can't quite believe it's a real town."

"Oh, no," Lucas assured her. "I believe in it. We have such towns in Brandusa. They contain nothing but fields of barley and herds of bored, mischief-making goats."

Journey laughed again.

"We have a great deal in common," Lucas said. As she had told him of Lummox, he'd been both caught up in her story and comparing it to his own. "I too felt stifled in the place of my birth."

She glanced around the room incredulously, making Lucas see its magnificence with her eyes. "You *did*?"

"I did indeed," he assured her. "But I've forgotten my manners. I will tell you my story, but first, may I offer you a drink? A gentleman should never let a lady stand thirsty."

A fetching pink blush colored her cheeks. "I forgot my manners too. And after all the work Mrs. Florescu did teaching them to me! I didn't do the proper introduction. And with a prince, too!" Curtsying again, she said, "I am honored to meet you, Prince Lucas."

"Please, just call me Lucas," he said immediately. She stared at him as if he had lost his wits. He probably had. He could think of nothing but that he had finally, *finally* found his mate. But she was still staring, so he offered the first explanation that came to mind. "We may be more casual on this special occasion."

"Yes." She stifled a sigh, then drew herself up into a more formal posture. "Of course."

Fool, roared his dragon. *The* special occasion *is your engagement to another woman!*

Lucas opened his mouth to assure her that there would be no

engagement. Then he closed it. Journey was American. She would know nothing of mates, or of the customs of either royalty or dragons. More importantly, she didn't know *him*.

If he blurted out that he really was a dragon and he'd known at first sight that she was his true love, she'd think he was a lunatic.

If he took her outside and shifted to prove it, he'd terrify her.

If he told her he was going to refuse the engagement because he'd met her and that Raluca would be thrilled, she'd think he was lying to seduce her.

Lucas frowned, trying to think of the best option. Perhaps he should simply continue getting to know her for another hour or so, then take her to meet Raluca. He and Raluca could explain together that neither of them chose the engagement and they were not going to go through with it. Then he'd be free to court Journey. They could get to know each other as men and women normally did. Once he was certain that she wouldn't think he was a madman or a monster, he would explain everything.

Journey didn't seem to have noticed his long hesitation. She appeared to have become depressed at the mention of his engagement, which gave him a strange mixture of feelings. On the one hand, he wished he could tell her the truth immediately. On the other hand, he was glad that she clearly wished he wasn't about to marry someone else.

Smoothly, Lucas said, "May I offer you the traditional drink of the royal family of Brandusa?"

Journey brightened a little at that. With an inner wince of recognition, he saw that she was trying to enjoy what she could in a situation she wished could be different. He knew all too much about that.

"Yes, please," she said. "I love traditional things."

"I can see. You wear our gown and shoes beautifully." He turned to the bartender. "Two flutes of dragonfire."

"Oooh…" Journey breathed. "That sounds exciting."

The bartender reverently took the bottle from beneath the bar and poured out two flutes. The orange-red liquor roiled in the glasses like liquid flame, seething and sending up wisps of smoke before it settled.

"What's it made of?" Journey asked.

"See if you can guess after you try it." He offered her a glass, then took his. "There is a toast in three parts. You drink after each one.

33

Match your sips to mine, so you finish on the third."

She nodded eagerly, then inhaled the air over her glass. "It smells like... I know it, but I can't put my finger on it..."

"Like fire?" Lucas asked. "Like hot metal?"

"Yes! I've never had a drink that smells like that." She glanced into the glass. Lucas was secretly amused to see her visibly wonder if it would taste revolting, then resolve to be polite no matter what.

"The toast," he reminded her, holding up his glass, and she raised hers to meet his. "We raise our glasses to the three treasures of the dragon. To honor."

"To honor," Journey echoed, and drank with him.

It was impossible to get used to the taste of dragonfire. The liquor tasted of fire, of peaches plucked on a summer day, of dreams and hopes and desire. It curled like flames over the tongue and slid down the throat like molten gold.

Lucas felt the fire of the liquor spread throughout his body. He had to alter his stance; he'd gotten so hard, his breeches were tight. Dragonfire wasn't an aphrodisiac, exactly; it wouldn't make you desire someone if you didn't already. If you drank it with friends or family, it brought on a pleasant nostalgia for all the good times you'd shared. But if you drank it with a lover, the evening was likely to conclude with a wild night of passion.

Journey's eyes widened as she swallowed. She took a deep breath, making her ivory breasts move within the corset. A very light sweat sprang up, giving her exposed skin a lovely glow. She looked Lucas boldly over from head to foot, her eyes lingering at the bulge in his breeches, then hastily jerked her gaze back to his face.

He raised his glass again. "To gold."

"To gold," Journey repeated, and they both drank again.

She licked a scarlet droplet from her lips. Lucas watched her tongue moisten her full lips, and imagined it flicking against his. Tasting and caressing its way down his body. Tracing the dragonmarks on his belly and chest. Then licking further down...

He forced his mind away from those images, and lifted his glass for the final toast. "To the open sky."

No dragon could have spoken the final toast with more longing than Journey as she repeated, "To the open sky."

They drained their glasses. The dragonfire burned its way down his throat, sending tendrils of heat coiling around his limbs. Its flavor lingered on his lips, and its perfume surrounded him.

"I can still taste it," whispered Journey.

She leaned in as she spoke, making him long to bend down and taste it on her lips. Lucas felt dizzy, as if he was floating in flames, and couldn't tell if it was the dragonfire or being so close to Journey. She was barely a handspan away from him. He could feel the heat of her body. It was maddening that he couldn't touch her.

Then he realized that there was a way that he could.

"Dance with me," he said, and offered her his hand.

Her warm fingers closed over his. That simple contact was more arousing than caressing the naked bodies of any of his previous partners. He had to take a deep breath to steady himself before he stepped out with her on to the dance floor.

The orchestra was playing a slow waltz. Lucas put his palm on her back and began to lead her. Her skirts whispered against his legs and her breasts brushed against his chest. He could feel every breath she took. The perfume of the dragonfire still hung about them as they moved together as easily as if they'd been dance partners all their lives.

"What was that drink?" Journey asked. Her voice was soft, pitched to carry only to him. "I've never tasted anything like it."

"Shall I tell you, or do you want a chance to guess?"

"Some kind of fruit brandy? Not pear... Not plum... Not cherry..." With a mischievous smile, she guessed, "The forbidden fruit?"

"Very good! Yes, it's brandy distilled from forbidden fruits." He'd tell her later that the aged brandy was then finished with a breath of actual dragonfire.

Journey's eyebrows rose. "Come on, what is it really?"

"But that's exactly..." Then Lucas realized the nature of her misunderstanding, and laughed. "It's not the actual forbidden fruit from the Garden of Eden. It's a native fruit that's called after it because it's so delicious and rare. It's only ripe for about two weeks in the height of summer."

Journey laughed as well. "Oh! Well, no wonder I didn't know about it. I've never been here in summer; I only arrived three months ago."

"Directly from..." Lucas had to pause to recall the strange name.

"Lummox?"

"I love the way you say it," she said with a grin. "It sounds exactly the way I feel about it. No, I traveled in other parts of Europe for nine months before I ended up here. I was originally only going to stay for a couple weeks, but I got an offer for a more long-term job. And I really like it here."

"There is much to love," Lucas replied. He meant it. But he also wished he could love it as uncomplicatedly as she.

His tone must have said more than he had, because she replied, "Of course, it's easy to love a place when you're just visiting. It's different when you have history there."

Lucas nodded, but did not reply. Journey didn't speak again, but the silence wasn't awkward. Their conversation seemed to continue, but in the motion of their bodies rather than in words. Couples moved and swirled around them, but Lucas felt as if they were dancing alone. They seemed to float across the dance floor, as if they were waltzing in mid-air. Nothing existed but the warmth of Journey's body in his, the sound of her breath, the fire in his blood, and joy of moving in harmony.

Then Journey sighed, her breasts moving against his chest. "I shouldn't monopolize you like this. I know you're supposed to dance with as many women as you can. In fact, I know who you should dance with next! There's a girl who's about to turn eighteen, who'd get the thrill of a lifetime—"

Lucas followed Journey's gaze until it settled on a pretty young girl in a crimson gown waltzing in the arms of an equally young man. He was a graceful dancer. The girl's eyes were closed, an expression of utter bliss on her face, as he guided her across the floor.

"I do not think she wishes to be interrupted," Lucas said, relieved at the easy excuse to stay with Journey. "Not even for the good luck of dancing with me."

"I think you're right." Journey too sounded relieved. "Looks like she's had her good luck already."

The orchestra finished the waltz, and Lucas brought them to a graceful halt.

He released her hand, stepped back, and turned to the orchestra. Catching the eye of the conductor, he made a small gesture of his hand:

Another.

The conductor nodded, and the orchestra struck up another waltz.

Lucas bowed and offered her his hand again. "May I have the next dance?"

With a delighted smile, Journey curtsied. "You may."

Their second dance was as enchanting as their first. So was their third. And their fourth. The conductor caught on to Lucas's intent, and had the orchestra play only tunes that would be easy for a foreigner — waltzes and folk tunes whose simple dances could easily be learned on the fly by a good dancer with a strong partner.

Lucas and Journey danced and talked, mostly about her travels. Her favorite place in Europe, outside of Brandusa, was Venice; his favorite was Vienna. The coincidence of the V amused them in a manner Lucas recognized from seeing other new couples' delight at sharing some trivial similarity. He'd once heard Ellie and Hal enraptured by the discovery that they both loved root beer and hated Dr. Pepper. Lucas had thought it a ridiculous topic for a fifteen-minute conversation. Now he understood.

As their fourth dance concluded, Lucas stepped back. As he began to bow and offer Journey his hand, a cold voice said, "Your highness?"

Lucas straightened and turned. Grand Duke Vaclav stood on one side of him, and Raluca's uncle, Duke Constantine, on the other. Grand Duke Vaclav wore a familiar expression of chilly disapproval, while Duke Constantine seemed to be repressing outright anger.

"It is good luck to dance with the prince. It is not better luck to dance with the prince *four times.*" Grand Duke Vaclav shot a contemptuous glance at Journey, making Lucas's blood flash into steam.

"*I* asked *her* to dance," Lucas replied, trying to keep his voice even. "You will address your concerns to *me.*"

Duke Constantine broke in, "Princess Raluca, *your betrothed,* is charming the people of Brandusa with her efforts to meet and dance with the guests."

Lucas was watching Journey, not Duke Constantine. When the duke mentioned Raluca, Journey flinched as if she'd been slapped.

"I'm sorry," she said, looking from Duke Constantine to Grand Duke Vaclav to Lucas. "Lu—Prince Lucas, it was wonderful to meet you. I'll never forget it. And I won't keep you any longer."

She stepped back, her lovely green eyes clouded with sorrow.

Fool, Lucas's dragon roared. *You missed your chance to explain. Now our mate is leaving us. Quick, stop her before it's too late!*

Hot blood rushed to Lucas's head. His dragon was so loud, he could barely hear himself think. How dare Grand Duke Vaclav look at his mate with such contempt! How dare Duke Constantine try to separate them!

"Grand Duke Vaclav, Duke Constantine, leave us. Now!" Lucas put the chill of command into his voice.

The men gave him a final pair of glares, then marched off. Journey started to follow them.

Lucas caught her hand. "Journey, stay with me."

To his dismay, she eyed him warily. "No, they're right. I should go. It's your engagement ball."

Lucas gritted his teeth. All his careful planning had evaporated in a puff of smoke. Now he had to explain quickly, before he lost her trust forever. "Journey, wait. It's an arranged marriage. Raluca and I don't love each other."

She detached her hand from his grip. "I'm sorry, but that's between you and the princess. And I'm sorry I led you on. I don't know what I was thinking—I got carried away. But I have to go now."

Stop her! His dragon's roar nearly deafened him.

"No, wait! It's not what you think!" Lucas heard his voice rise, louder than he'd intended. He never sounded like that, ever—out of control, frantic—but he couldn't stop himself. "Now that I've met you, there won't be any engagement. I love *you*, Journey. Raluca will understand—"

The look Journey gave him made him feel like he'd been stabbed in the heart. Worse. She looked like he'd stabbed *her* in the heart.

"I'm so stupid," she said quietly, more to herself than to him. "You can run away from home, but you can never run away from yourself. I swore I'd never again fall for a charming liar, and here I am with another one."

The pain in her voice struck Lucas dumb. Before he could say anything, she went on, "And my job! I completely forgot why I'm even here!"

She looked around wildly, then bolted across the dance floor. Lucas took a step toward her.

"Are you all right?" It was a voice like crystal. Raluca stood beside him, looking concerned. "I saw you having some sort of confrontation with Grand Duke Vaclav and my uncle, and then a red-headed woman ran away…"

"That 'red-headed woman' was my mate!"

"Oh!" Raluca first looked shocked, then delighted. "Lucas, how wonderful! But where did she go?"

Lucas followed her gaze. Journey was gone.

CHAPTER FOUR
Journey

Journey fled across the dance floor, trying and failing to keep tears from her eyes.

The ball had turned on a dime from being the best night of her life to one of the worst. How could she have forgotten, even for an hour, that charming Prince Lucas was about to get engaged? How could she have let herself slip from enjoying his company as one of the many lucky women who got to meet the prince, to flirting with him—wanting him—imagining that she could have him?

But the worst part had been when she'd realized that she *could* have him… if she was willing to sacrifice her integrity for a sleazy fling with a silver-tongued cheater.

Ugh! Ugh! Ugh!

Journey angrily dashed the tears from her eyes. And, momentarily blinded, she tripped over someone's foot.

"Sorry," she gasped, her arms flying out to catch herself.

Several people grabbed her before she could fall. But her foot came down hard and at an angle against the marble floor. The wooden heel of her left shoe snapped off.

"Oh, goddammit!" Journey exclaimed.

She took off her shoes and picked them up along with the heel, then stood barefoot on the cold floor, looking around for Stefania. She was nowhere to be seen. But near where Journey had seen her last was a small door, presumably to one of the side rooms Mrs. Florescu had warned her about.

Journey bolted for the door, then flung it open.

The room was exactly what she had imagined: very small but luxuriously furnished, with a velvet loveseat just big enough for two. Stefania and the young man she'd been dancing with all night were draped over it and each other, kissing passionately.

"Stefania!" Journey exclaimed.

The couple sprang apart, looking flushed and guilty.

Normally Journey would have simply told them to get back on the dance floor. But now, with her own misery and frustrated passion and longing to get as far away from Lucas as possible swirling within her, she snapped, "Stefania, this is exactly what your parents forbade. Come with me. We're going home."

"Noooooo," Stefania wailed. "One more dance!"

The young man stepped forward. He was no older than Stefania, from the looks of him, but more self-possessed. "It's my fault. I'm sorry. We'll stay on the dance floor."

"The dance is over. Come on." Journey caught Stefania by the hand.

The young man snatched up Stefania's free hand, gave it a hasty kiss, and said, "I'll call on you tomorrow. Don't worry, I can charm even the fiercest mother."

This seemed to console Stefania, who cast him a coquettish smile over her shoulder. "You needn't ask permission from my parents, Doru. Tomorrow I'll be eighteen!"

Journey hurried Stefania outside, past the guards and down the marble steps, and into their waiting carriage. She felt worse and worse as the coach clattered across the cobblestones. She'd not only ruined her own evening, she'd also ruined Stefania's. Journey could have simply extracted her from the private room—she hadn't needed to drag Stefania away from the ball. It had been wrong of her to take her own unhappiness out on her charge. As for her own feelings, she could suck them up for one more hour.

Journey wiped her eyes again. Once she got control of her breath, she'd turn the carriage around. Then she saw that while she still had the heel in her hand, she'd dropped the broken dancing shoe.

It was the last straw. Journey burst into tears.

"Journey!" Stefania exclaimed. "Whatever is the matter?"

Journey couldn't bring herself to confess what had happened between her and Prince Lucas. Instead, she gasped out, "I broke the heel on one of your mother's shoes and then I lost it... And I was mean to you... And I have to leave Brandusa and go back to Lummox and I don't know if I can ever come back!"

Stefania hugged her. "Oh, Journey, my mother won't care about the shoes. And I forgive you. And you'll come back some day, I know you will. If I marry Doru, we'll keep a guest room just for you!"

Journey hugged Stefania back. Whatever else happened, at least she had a friend. "Thanks. I'll take you up on that some day. Listen, Stefania, I don't want go back to the ball. I... um... I'd be embarrassed to go barefoot. But I shouldn't have taken you away. You turn eighteen at midnight, and it's almost midnight now. If you swear on your honor that you'll stay in the ballroom and come home once the ball is over, I'll let you go back."

"I swear on my honor," Stefania said instantly, touching her fingers to her temples where a crown would press.

The coach pulled up in front of the Florescus' house. Journey got out, gave the coachman his instructions, and waved goodbye to Stefania. The coach clattered away, back to the palace.

Journey went inside the darkened home. She sat down on her bed, but couldn't imagine sleeping. Finally, she put on a pair of her own shoes and went back outside to get some fresh air.

The neighborhood was especially beautiful in the moonlight. The steepled roofs and narrow roads were like an illustration from a fairytale.

She was all alone. Brandusans were not often night owls, and everyone was either asleep or at the ball. But she wasn't afraid. She knew the neighborhood well. It was very safe, and if anyone bothered her, one scream would send everyone rushing out of their houses.

Lost in thought, Journey walked and walked until, with a start, she realized that she had left the houses behind. She'd walked all the way to the broad main road that ran between the residential neighborhoods and the woods that bordered the river.

She glanced into the woods. They were dark, but not too dark to walk through on this bright night. And she'd like to see the river by moonlight, one last time.

Journey made her way through the woods and to the sandy

riverbank. There she stood a while in thought, looking out at the shimmering waters. When it had become clear that she wouldn't find another job, the Florescus had invited her to stay in their home as a guest for the week after Stefania turned eighteen. She had agreed at the time, but all she wanted now was to make a clean break—with Brandusa, with her year of travel and freedom, and with Lucas.

As soon as the sun rose, she'd go to the airport and get on the first flight back to America.

CHAPTER FIVE
Lucas

Lucas looked wildly around the ballroom. Journey was nowhere to be seen.

He'd finally, *finally* met his mate, and she'd been so much more wonderful than he'd ever imagined. And she'd decided that he was a liar and a cheater, and fled from him as if he was her worst nightmare.

Lucas buried his face in his hands and groaned.

Then he pulled himself together. He could still convince her. She might not believe him, but surely she'd believe Raluca.

He quickly explained what had happened, then said, "Come with me. I'll find her and then you can help me explain about the engagement."

They hurried across the dance floor in the direction he'd last seen Journey running, but she was nowhere to be found. Finally, they went outside and asked the guards at the doors if they'd seen a red-haired woman leave.

"Yes, your highness," replied a guard. "I tried to stop her, but she and her companion jumped into a carriage and left."

"Her companion?" asked Raluca.

"A very young woman in a red dress," replied the guard.

"Why did you try to stop her?" Lucas inquired.

"She dropped her shoe." The guard held up a dancing shoe of black wood and green leather. "She was barefoot and carrying them—see, the heel is broken off."

Lucas took the shoe, running his fingers over the polished wood and soft leather. As a memento of Journey, the ordinary object felt unexpectedly precious to him.

Mischievously, Raluca suggested, "Now all you need to do is have every woman in the kingdom try it on and see who it fits."

Lucas wasn't in the mood for jokes. "That won't be necessary. I know who she is." To the guard, he said, "Show me the guest list."

Out of the corner of his eye, he saw the guards all looking incredibly curious. Raluca noticed too, and haughtily informed them, "The crown prince of Brandusa takes a personal interest in the welfare of every single one of his subjects. Even an ordinary guest whom he merely spotted running away as if something had upset her. Of course he wishes to know what went wrong for her at his ball."

The guards hastily said, "Of course, your highness," and "Very kind, your highness," and "Didn't mean to look nosy, your highness."

One of them shoved the guest list at him, eyes averted. Lucas scanned the list until he found her: Journey Jacobson, guest of Stefania Florescu. He memorized her address, which was in a quiet neighborhood near the river.

Even out of the ballroom, Lucas felt smothered and spied-on and claustrophobic. The guards' fixed stares at anywhere but him only made him feel their presence more acutely.

"Let us take a stroll around the garden," he suggested.

"What a lovely idea," Raluca replied. "It's such a beautiful night."

He led her into the winter garden. In its own season it was a popular place to stroll, with the quince trees in full red bloom, shining against the snow like bursts of flame. In spring it was a dull place with nothing in flower. No one else was likely to go there, which made it an excellent location for a private talk.

The night was cool and the moon was nearly full. A brisk breeze blew, making Raluca's skirts flutter. For the first time since Lucas's dance had been interrupted, he felt his head clear.

"You found your mate, Lucas. I'm so happy for you!" Hesitantly, Raluca asked, "What's it really like?"

All the shock and joy and wonder of that first sight of Journey came back to him with almost as much force as when it had happened. "Like nothing you can imagine. I don't know how to describe it. I think it's something you have to experience to understand."

Wistfully, Raluca said, "I hope I do, some day."

"Now that you don't have to marry me, you probably will."

"Perhaps." She didn't look as happy as he'd expected. "Or perhaps a marriage will be arranged between me and one of your cousins. My uncle is very determined to have this alliance go through."

"So is my great-uncle," Lucas said with a sigh. He wanted to tell her to refuse a second arrangement. But he knew all too well that it was not so simple.

Two voices spoke at once from behind them.

"Lucas." The cold voice belonged to Grand Duke Vaclav.

"Raluca!" The angry voice belonged to Duke Constantine.

Lucas and Raluca turned around. And faced not only his great-uncle and Raluca's uncle, but King Andrei and Queen Livia.

Only Queen Livia managed a smile. "I understand the desire to snatch a moment alone, my dears, but it's nearly midnight. You must hurry back for the ring ceremony."

Lucas stood up straight and tall, deliberately looming over the lot of them. With a strange mixture of satisfaction and nervous anticipation, he said, "There won't be any ring ceremony. I just met my mate. The arrangement is off."

Everyone broke into a discordant chorus of angry or shocked or denying exclamations.

"Be quiet and listen!" Lucas heard the command in his own voice. Everyone fell silent in an instant.

For the second time that night, he recounted his meeting with Journey, and how she'd misunderstood his intentions and fled. While the king and queen clearly had mixed feelings, which Lucas could guess was a combination of happiness for him and alarm at the political fallout, Grand Duke Vaclav and Duke Constantine looked ready to spontaneously combust with rage.

The king was the first to speak. "But Lucas, you cannot break the arrangement simply by telling us that you found your mate. You must bring her to the palace and have her state her intention to marry you."

Lucas had forgotten about that part. His jaw clenched so hard, his teeth hurt. Journey would hardly agree to get engaged *tonight*. He'd be lucky if she even gave him a chance to explain tonight!

"Surely I can be allowed a grace period, given that I've already found her," Lucas pointed out. "I can't do the ring ceremony with Raluca knowing that I already have a mate, then produce her later and break the engagement."

"Indeed he cannot," Raluca chimed in. "How humiliating for me. Under the circumstances, I refuse to do the ring ceremony."

Their relatives all looked at each other, seeming to reach some silent agreement. Then King Andrei turned back to Lucas. "I give you one month to get engaged to your mate. If you can do that, the entire arrangement is off. If you can't, you marry Raluca."

"But my mate is human," Lucas protested. "And American! She'll think it's too soon."

Queen Livia patted his shoulder. "My dear, simply explain it to her. She'll see the necessity of an early commitment."

Lucas forced himself not to make any further protests. Arranged marriages were normal for them. It would make no sense to them if he said, "But it's not fair to her to pressure her like that."

"Very well," he said.

"I agree," said Raluca. "Lucas, she is your mate. You're destined to be together. But don't chase after her tonight. Let her sleep on it. Then get her address from the guest list, and we'll both visit her tomorrow. I'll help you explain about the engagement."

Much as Lucas longed to rush to Journey right now, he had to admit that Raluca's idea was less likely to make her flee in horror. Again. "Good idea."

"And what do we say to the guests at your engagement ball?" Grand Duke Vaclav asked icily.

If the entire city began chattering about Journey being Lucas's mate before he got a chance to properly court her, she'd probably catch the first plane back to America.

"Raluca, could we claim that you fell ill?" Lucas asked. "We could say it's not serious, but you don't want to get engaged when you're not feeling well."

"If it will get me out of this marriage, I'll faint in full view of the entire ballroom." She winked at Lucas as if she was looking forward to it.

"Raluca!" Duke Constantine snapped. "It is your duty as a princess to marry to benefit your country, not yourself."

"To benefit *you*," Lucas muttered. Louder, he said, "Fainting will not be necessary. You can return to the palace through a different entrance. I'll make the announcement."

Raluca ran off, her skirts trailing behind her like a flag. Lucas suppressed a sigh. He didn't want to marry her any more than she wanted to marry him, but it was something of a blow to his vanity to have two women run away from him in a single night.

Lucas could feel the dukes' glares at his back as he returned to the ballroom. He waved the orchestra to silence, made his announcement, and left as quickly as possible, claiming that he had to go sit by Raluca's side.

It was an immense relief to get to his bedroom, dismiss his valet, and close the door behind him. He sat down on his bed, tired but hopeful. Tomorrow he'd see Journey again. He'd have Raluca with him to prove he wasn't trying to cheat on her. He'd be able to take his time explaining the situation, rather than babbling in an incoherent rush.

And he'd bring her an apology gift. By American standards, the normal dragon gifts of precious jewelry would be far too lavish. But he knew just the thing: a bottle of dragonfire. She'd enjoy that, he was certain. And she wouldn't know it cost its weight in gold.

Feeling much better, Lucas walked to the closet. He took out a pair of pajamas and started to unfold them to make sure they were new and would fit him, rather than being a relic from his teenage years.

Protect Journey!

Lucas dropped the pajamas, startled by his dragon's sudden roar.

"What?" Lucas asked aloud. "What's going on?"

Journey's in danger! Defend her!

Lucas didn't pause to ask how his dragon knew. His dragon could be reckless and hot-tempered and uncaring of human concerns, but Lucas knew instinctively, as surely as he knew that Journey was his mate, that his dragon was right.

He automatically looked for his gun before remembering that he'd left it in his apartment in America. He was in Brandusa now, where guns were so thoroughly banned that even criminals didn't have them.

Then he saw the sword hanging on the wall. In the instant it took him to grab it, he hoped he hadn't forgotten how to use it. Then his hand closed around the hilt. It was as familiar as a lifelong friend, as familiar as Journey's eyes.

Lucas buckled on his sword and turned toward the door.

There is no time, said his dragon. *Fly!*

Lucas ran across the room and threw open the window. He hesitated, looking at the ground five stories below. He'd never transformed in midair before. If he was too slow, he'd fall to his death.

He leaped out into the night. For a terrifying instant, he was a man plummeting through the air. Then he was a dragon, straining to catch the wind beneath his wings and arrest his fall. The tip of his tail touched the ground, and then he was skimming over the garden, his powerful wings taking him up and out, over the palace walls.

Lucas concentrated to make himself invisible, then flew on. The moon shone full, casting a silvery light over the sleeping city. It was easy to spot the Florescu's neighborhood, though he'd have to land to find the house itself.

But as he started to search for an open square where he'd have room to touch down, his dragon instincts urged him further on, past the homes and to the woods beside the riverbank. Why would Journey be in trouble in that remote area, in the middle of the night?

He supposed he'd find out. He landed as close as he could to the area where he instinctively knew she was, touching down on the empty road beside the woods. Once he became a man, his instincts were less sharp. But where instinct left off, training took over.

Lucas drew his sword and slipped into the woods, moving silently, all his senses alert and focused. His mate was in danger. He would protect her with his life. Nothing else mattered.

CHAPTER SIX
Journey

Journey stood gazing at the rushing river. The moonlight turned it to liquid silver. She tried to fix the sight into her memory, so she could treasure it always.

There was a sharp crack behind her like a branch snapping underfoot. Journey jumped, then turned around.

She saw nothing but the woods. But she had a sense that something... or someone... was watching her from within them. It was probably a deer; they were big enough to snap a branch if they stepped on it. But her back crept.

Though she felt foolish, she called out, "Hello? Is someone there?"

There was no reply. No sound.

Deer were active at dawn and dusk, not in the middle of the night. And an animal would have run and made more noise when she'd shouted.

Journey's sense of uneasiness increased. She might have bad instincts when it came to men who were dangerous to her heart, but she was an excellent judge of physical safety. Her rule of thumb for traveling alone was to listen to her gut and trust that if something made her nervous, there was probably a reason. That rule had kept her safe so far.

Her gut told her now that she was in deadly peril.

She would have screamed, but the noise of the river would drown out her voice. Instead, Journey yanked up her skirts in both hands, then bolted along the narrow riverbank. There was a stone bridge further on, which led to more woods, and then another residential neighborhood. If she could get across the bridge—

"After her!" The voice was rough and male. "Quick, she's getting away!"

Adrenaline surged through Journey's blood. She dared one quick glance over her shoulder as she ran, her heart pounding.

Six men in black cloth masks had emerged from the woods. Their brandished swords glinted sharp and deadly in the moonlight. And they were gaining on her.

Journey tore along the riverbank, her breath searing her lungs. But though she ran as fast as she could, the footsteps behind her came closer with every step she took. Terror nearly stopped her heart. She'd never make it to the bridge. If she jumped into the river, with its treacherous undercurrents, she'd probably be swept away and drown. But at least she'd have a chance. She started to turn toward the water.

Another man stepped out of the woods in front of her, sword in hand.

A shriek burst from Journey's throat. Then she recognized him. Her scream changed into a choked gasp of surprise. It was Lucas.

"Go over the bridge!" He gestured behind him with his free hand. "I'll protect you."

Journey ran past him, her chest heaving for breath. The men chasing her shouted in anger and confusion, but the blood was pounding so hard in her ears that she couldn't understand the words. Her feet slammed into hard stone. She'd reached the bridge.

Halfway along its short span, she heard Lucas's voice rise above the tumult. "Surrender, or I'll burn you to ash and gone!"

Burn? Journey thought. *With a sword?*

Out of all the bizarre events of the last few minutes, that was so strange that it stopped her in her tracks. Gasping for breath, she turned around.

Lucas held the masked men at bay. There were six of them to one of him, but none of them moved to attack him. But they still held their swords at the ready. They seemed to be at a stand-off.

Even in the terror and shock of the moment, Journey was struck by how magnificent he looked. His hair and the embroidered dragons on his tunic shone like platinum, his jewelry of gold and diamonds glittered in the moonlight, and he stood poised with a deadly grace. She had no doubt that he could strike like lightning.

"Who sent you?" Lucas demanded.

The fury in his voice would have terrified anyone, and she saw several of the men flinch. But none replied.

Lucas spoke more softly, but with an even more frightening chill in his voice. "Who sent you?"

The men still didn't speak, though they shifted uncomfortably.

"I see," said Lucas. "I would recognize your voices. Or your accents, perhaps. But you only delay the inevitable. You know you cannot fight me. Surrender."

Is he really that good? Journey wondered. *Is any swordfighter good enough to fight six to one?*

She bit her lip, trying to figure out what she should do. Run and get help? Stay so she could help if a fight started? She wasn't armed, but maybe she could throw something and distract them. Journey looked around for throwing material, but saw nothing.

"I have made two calls for surrender," Lucas said. "This is your last chance. Surrender, or face the dragon!"

One of the masked men lunged to the side, trying to dart into the woods. As Lucas's sword flashed down to bar his way, another man moved his bare hand as if he was throwing something at Lucas. Journey couldn't see what he held, but clear liquid glittered in the air.

Lucas ducked, but some of whatever it was must have hit him. Though nothing else had touched him, he let out a cry of surprise and pain.

Acid? Journey thought, horrified.

Instantly, four of the men attacked Lucas. While he was distracted fighting them, the other two vanished into the woods. Lucas's sword moved too fast for Journey's eyes to follow, flashing like a silver streak. The clash of steel rose up above the sound of the rushing waters. First one masked man, then another dropped his sword with a yelp. Both backed away, their sword arms hanging limp, clearly disabled.

Two men emerged from the woods behind Lucas.

"Behind you!" Journey yelled.

Lucas dropped down in a graceful lunge. A sword whistled over his head with barely an inch to spare. Lucas leaped toward the river, but two men moved to bar his way.

He struck out in a lightning thrust. One assassin fell into the river and was instantly carried away. Then the remaining three men attacked Lucas simultaneously. He spun, first parrying a sword cut to the head and then a thrust to the back, but the third man got through his guard. Lucas didn't flinch or make a sound, but a wet dark stain appeared across the front of his tunic.

The remaining assassins closed in on him.

But Journey hadn't been standing idle while Lucas fought. Even as she was watching the battle, terrified that he'd be killed on her behalf, she'd been prying at the loose stones of the waist-high guard wall of the bridge. The bridge was old, the mortar crumbling. Her nails broke and her fingers bled, but she finally managed to get one stone loose. It was a lump of granite as big as a brick.

Journey hurled the rock at the nearest enemy. It hit him square in the back, knocking him to his knees.

Then Lucas was left fighting the last two men. All three moved so fast that their swords were bright streaks in the air. She couldn't tell if any of the attackers had been wounded; they all wore black. But another dark stain appeared on Lucas's tunic, making Journey's heart lurch. She couldn't bear to take her eyes off the fight, as if he might be killed if she stopped watching over him. But as she watched, she felt around for another loose stone in the wall.

One of the enemies jumped back, then kicked sand into Lucas's face. Lucas kept his guard up, but stumbled backward. While he was distracted, the man grabbed the enemy Journey had knocked down, dragging him to his feet, and fled into the woods with him. The rest of the assassins followed.

Journey listened to them retreating through the woods, leaves rustling and twigs snapping underfoot, until the sounds faded into the distance. Just like that, the assassins were gone. Lucas and Journey were alone.

Lucas turned to her. "Are you hurt?"

"I'm fine," she said, though her voice shook. "But *you're* not!"

"Oh…" Lucas glanced down at himself. Blood was soaking through his tunic, but he seemed more embarrassed than concerned. "I'm out of practice. It's been five years since I last fought with a sword."

He swayed where he stood. Journey ran to him and caught him by the shoulders. "Sit down."

"No—"

"Yes. You're about to collapse."

"I'm not." He straightened, lifting his chin in a lordly manner. Then his gaze softened, and she saw him swallow. "I *can't*. Not yet. I have to get you to safety first."

Journey had seen his charm and sensuality at the ball, and his courage and protective fierceness in the battle. Now she caught a glimpse of his vulnerability. It made her heart squeeze painfully.

"How about we both get to safety, huh?" she suggested. "Let's walk across the bridge. We can knock on someone's door and call for an ambulance."

He dug in his heels when she tried to tug him toward the bridge. "Those men were after *you*. I have to stay with you to protect you."

She couldn't believe that the prince had not only saved her life, but seemed intent on appointing himself her personal bodyguard. Maybe he was trying to make up for upsetting her at the ball.

"Thank you, but the police can protect me." *Until I catch a flight back to America*, she thought, but that hurt too much to say aloud. "And you need a doctor."

Lucas reached out and cupped her cheek in his hand. Journey drew in a breath. The warmth of his touch tingled through her whole body, and the intensity of his gaze caught her like a butterfly in amber.

"Journey, I know I've seemed to be a man without honor," he said. "But you've seen for yourself that I'll put my body between you and danger. Will you trust me to take you to a place where you'll be safe?"

His chiseled features were white and taut with pain, his tunic wet and dark all down the front. Whatever else he'd done, he'd come close to death for her.

"Yes," Journey replied. "I trust you."

"This is not how I wanted to tell you," he muttered. Then, with a resigned shrug, he said, "You know those local legends about the royal family turning into dragons?"

"Yes."

"They're true." Lucas spoke as if he didn't expect to be believed.

Journey didn't doubt him for an instant. His voice held the

unmistakable ring of truth. But more than that, it didn't seem impossible that the golden-haired prince who had defended her against assassins was every bit as astonishing as he seemed. Of course he could turn into a dragon. Of course magic was real. She'd always wanted to believe that there was more to the world than simple known facts. On some level, she had always believed.

"I knew it!" Journey exclaimed.

Lucas's eyebrows rose in surprise. "You believe me?"

The entire town of Lummox, North Dakota would think she was a gullible idiot if they could hear her now. Journey didn't care. "One hundred percent."

His tension and weariness eased, and his sensual lips parted in a faint smile. Then he said the last thing she expected. "I have to wash my face."

He knelt at the edge of the river and splashed water over his face, scrubbing hard. She was baffled until she remembered how one of the attackers had thrown some liquid in his face and he'd reacted as if it had hurt him.

When he straightened up, she anxiously peered at his face, but saw no mark on it. "What did that guy throw on you? Pepper spray?"

Lucas shook his head. "Dragonsbane. It wouldn't do anything to you. But it stops me from shifting."

"It looked like it hurt."

"It does. When I was a boy, my great-uncle, Grand Duke Vaclav, would sometimes dip our practice swords in it and have us fight with our shirts off, so any hits we took would feel like real wounds."

Journey recalled the Grand Duke with dislike. "When you say boy, how old are you talking about?"

"Since I was eleven."

"What an asshole!"

"He didn't do it to be sadistic. You need to learn to take a blow seriously, and you need to learn to fight while you're in pain. His training saved my life and yours tonight." Then Lucas gave her a wry smile, softening the angular planes of his face. "But you're right. He's an asshole."

Journey tried to smile with him, but she was having a hard time thinking of anything but all that blood.

"Can I take off your shirt?" Heat rose to her face as she heard her own words. "I mean, to tear it up for bandages."

"You may see to my wounds when we arrive. And don't worry so much about me. Shifters heal quickly." Lucas touched her hand. Even the slightest skin-to-skin contact with him sent a shock of pleasure through her body. "I'm going to become a dragon. Don't be frightened—What am I saying? You stood with me unarmed against six assassins with swords."

"I wasn't unarmed," Journey pointed out. "I had a big rock."

"And you made excellent use of it," Lucas said, his tone lightening. "Thank you for saving my life."

"Thank *you* for saving mine."

The riverbank was silent except for the sound of the rushing waters. Lucas's amber eyes were bleached silver by the moonlight. The blood on his tunic looked black.

Journey knew then, in her gut and in her heart, that he was not a man who cheated or lied. He'd seemed to be a sweet-talking cheater at the ball, but appearances could be deceiving. Good country boys could be liars and thieves. Small-town girls named Ashley could be world travelers named Journey. Princes could be dragons.

"Are you engaged?" she asked.

"No." His immediate reply was more convincing than any lengthy explanation. "It's complicated, but no."

"Are you in love with Princess Raluca?"

"No. And she's not in love with me, either. We're both trying to extract ourselves from an arrangement made by other people five years ago—an arrangement neither of us ever wanted."

"I believe you," Journey said. "I'm sorry I ran away from you without giving you a chance to explain. Now let's see you turn into a dragon!"

Though he was obviously still in pain, Lucas's startled grin made him look unexpectedly lighthearted and boyish. "I think I make things too complicated, sometimes. You make them so simple. Now stand aside. When I become a dragon, you can ride me. Don't worry about being seen. Once you get on my back, I'll make myself invisible."

"Invisible!" she breathed delightedly. "So it'll be like I'm riding on air?"

"I don't think so," Lucas replied. "I believe that even people who are not dragon shifters can see me if they're actually touching me. In any case, we will soon find out."

Journey stepped back.

The air around Lucas sparkled. Though the moonlight made everything else look black and white, the sparks around him glittered gold. He stood within a whirlwind of spinning fireflies. The golden cloud expanded, getting denser and denser until Lucas vanished from sight. Then it dispersed, and Journey stood before a dragon.

Like the sparks, the dragon was the only thing in the landscape that had color. It was pure gold, gleaming bright and true as the precious metal. She stared at the dragon, marveling. The membranes of his folded wings were thin as cloth, semi-transparent. His claws were sharp as golden daggers.

But he wasn't changed beyond all recognition. The man's wounds had transferred to the dragon, the bloody slashes shocking against his gleaming hide. And his eyes were Lucas's eyes, translucent amber. Even if she'd seen the dragon without warning or explanation, she felt like she would have known him.

Her entire life, Journey had always longed for magic to be real. As a child, she'd crammed herself into every closet in the house, forever hoping that this time the back would open into Narnia. When she got older, she gave up on magical doorways to other lands and instead pinned her dreams on airplanes that would take her away from Lummox.

And here she was, face to face with a dragon.

A dragon who was also the man who had saved her life.

A man who might be free to love her.

Journey mentally shook herself. She might believe in dragons, but she wasn't sure she believed in love at first sight. But she thought back to the look in his eyes when he'd first seen her, that bright regard like molten gold. To dancing with Lucas, and how they'd moved together like two bodies with a single heart. To how upset he'd gotten, his smooth charm shattering like glass, when that pair of horrible old men had marched up and tried to poison her mind against him. To Lucas squaring off against six assassins, placing his own body between her and danger.

The dragon spread out his magnificent wings, like sunlight made flesh. Then he reached out a claw and delicately tapped her shoulder.

Journey stepped around to the dragon's side, her thoughts whirling as fast as the glittering cloud that had surrounded Lucas. Did he really love her? Did she love him?

Did she *dare* love him?

Journey pushed those thoughts aside. She could worry about that later. Right now, she was going to get to ride a dragon!

The dragon offered her his bent forearm. She stepped on to it, then threw her leg over his back. Journey settled into a hollow behind his neck, big enough for her to fit into but small enough to hold her in place. She stroked his neck. The scales were smooth and soft, more like suede than snakeskin. A few blunt spines at his neck provided something for her to hold on to.

A huff of breath warned her to tighten her grip. Then the dragon leaped into the air. She gasped in surprise and wonder as they rose above the earth. The river became a thread of silver as the dragon soared higher. She could see the entire city spread out below her, a patchwork of buildings, roads, and forests. The castle gleamed in the center of the city, but she could see the towers and walls of other castles, some topping hills, some nestled in the woods.

Above her, the stars glittered like diamonds and the moon gleamed like a great pearl. The air was cold but bracing, with a faint scent of rain and pine. Journey had never felt more awake or alive, close to the stars and one with the night.

She supposed that Lucas must have made himself invisible by now, but he'd been correct that she could still see him. His wings steadily stroked the air. She knew he was in pain and weary, but his flight didn't show it. But she had the sense that flying made Lucas feel better, not worse. The thrill and joy she felt soaring through the air had to be felt by the dragon too. It didn't seem like the sort of thing it was possible to get tired of.

The three treasures of the dragon, she recalled Lucas saying. *Honor. Gold. And the open sky.*

They flew out of the city and into the countryside, then above a dense forest. The dragon began to spiral downward to where a castle's towers pierced the mass of trees. Down he flew, over the castle walls, and landed light as a feather on a courtyard on the roof.

Journey slid off and stepped back. Golden sparks gathered and spun around the dragon, then dispersed. Lucas was left standing on the courtyard, his sword buckled at his side and his tunic covered in drying blood.

"Please tell me there's a doctor here," Journey said.

"I'm afraid not," he admitted. "It's one of the royal family's winter retreats. This time of year, there's no one here but guards outside the walls and weekly caretakers. Nobody will even know we're here."

"But—"

He took her hand. "I told you, dragons heal quickly. I don't need anyone but you."

Journey drew in her breath, hearing a double meaning in his words. "Let's go inside. It's cold out here."

Lucas let her inside, then led her down a flight of stairs and into a hallway. The interior of the castle was the same blend of traditional lavishness with modern conveniences as she'd seen in the palace. The gold chandeliers had electric lights. As he'd said, it was absolutely empty. Their shoes echoed on the marble floors.

He opened a door to a luxurious suite, moved a painting aside to turn on the heat controls concealed behind it, and then headed straight for the bathroom. Journey started to hang back, but he said, "No, please come in."

Lucas had walked steadily and held his head high all the way down the stairs and along the corridor. But once he reached the bathroom, he sank down on the edge of an enormous sunken tub as if his legs had given way.

Journey put her arm around his shoulders, holding him steady, and was alarmed by how cold he felt. "You're freezing. You should take a hot bath."

"Later. There's medical supplies in the cabinet, I think." He gestured vaguely toward it. "Well, there were five years ago."

Journey opened it. The closet contained an interesting assortment of modern medical kits and witchy-looking wooden boxes filled with mysterious jars of herbs, labeled in spidery handwriting.

She started to reach for a first aid kit, then hesitated. "Do you want bandages and antiseptic, or possibly-magical herbs?"

That got a hint of a smile from Lucas. "Bandages and antiseptic, please. And one possibly-magical herb. Look for a bottle of liquid that says 'Heartsease.'"

Journey set the first aid kit on the floor, then began searching the witchy boxes for heartsease. "What's that?"

"The antidote to dragonsbane." He touched his cheek lightly, then jerked his fingers away as if he'd laid them on an open wound.

"I thought it washed off."

"It does, but that only makes it possible to shift. The pain remains until you take the antidote." Lucas spoke calmly, but she could hear the stress in his voice. "I'm lucky none got in my mouth."

"Is it poisonous?"

"Very. A small amount wouldn't kill you, but even a single swallowed drop would make you wish you were dead. In olden times it was used for torture." The tight control in Lucas's voice implied more pain than Journey liked to imagine.

She searched through the boxes until she finally found the heartsease. "Got it!"

He took the bottle and carefully tipped a few drops into his mouth. Almost immediately, a little color returned to his face, his stiff posture relaxed, and he gave a long sigh of relief. "That's better."

Journey stretched, shaking out her own tense muscles. She hadn't realized how much Lucas's pain had affected her until she saw it relieved. "Let me get your shirt off now."

She used a pair of scissors from the first aid kit to shear it off, exposing a lean but muscular chest smeared with drying blood and marked with an abstract pattern in glittering gold.

"You've got tattoos!" she exclaimed.

"You sound so shocked," Lucas teased. "Didn't you expect me to be... How do you say it...? Tatted in?"

"It's 'tatted out.' And no, I sure didn't." She started sponging the blood off his chest, exposing more of the golden tattoo. The intricate pattern covered his left shoulder and the left side of his upper chest. It was on his belly, too, fanning out symmetrically from his belly button.

"It's not a tattoo," Lucas admitted. "I was born with it. It's called dragonmarks. We all have them somewhere on our bodies, but the patterns are different. Unique. Like fingerprints."

Now that she'd cleaned the blood off, she could see where he was wounded. There was a slash near his right shoulder and another at his right side, but both had already started to close. They looked as if they had been inflicted the day before, not an hour ago.

Dragon magic, Journey thought with wonder.

She began cleaning his wounds with antiseptic. She'd never gotten any formal first aid training, but growing up in Lummox with the nearest doctor an hour's bumpy drive away, you learned to treat your own cuts and sprains.

His body grew warmer and warmer under her hands, until she wondered if he had a fever. Then remembered how hot he'd felt when she'd danced with him. "What's your normal temperature?"

"Thirty-nine degrees. That is, one hundred and two Fahrenheit. Dragons run hot."

"Thanks," Journey replied. "I know I should be used to Celsius by now, but I have to look it up every time. Well, I think you're back to normal now."

He nodded. "The chill was an effect of the dragonsbane."

Journey taped a bandage over the slash on his shoulder. Intent on her task, she forgot all the other questions she wanted to ask. Lucas too was silent, but Journey only noticed the quiet in the room when she finished and settled back to examine her work.

The taped-on bandages stood out stark white against Lucas's ivory skin and golden dragonmarks. They moved with each breath he took, just as the lean muscle of his chest and belly moved, and the dragonmarks glittered in the light. His shoulders and arms were more muscular than she'd realized when he'd had his tunic on. His hands were as beautiful as ever, but now she was close enough to see the corded tendons at his wrists and a few small scars across his knuckles.

In the ballroom, clothed and dancing, Lucas was every inch a prince, a sensual but unattainable fantasy. Half-naked and sitting in front of her, his skin still wet from the sponge she'd rubbed over his body, he seemed less elegant. More primal. She could feel the heat of his bare skin and smell a spicy scent that might be cologne or might just be him.

Slowly, she lifted her gaze to meet his eyes. They gleamed hot and bright, closer to gold than to topaz. He had looked at her like that at the ball, from across a crowded room. She hadn't understood what it meant, back then. She did now. He wanted her, as much as she wanted him.

"Lucas…" she whispered.

His voice was low and husky, unlike his usual polished tones. "I have wanted you since the moment I first laid eyes on you. When we danced at the ball, it was all I could do to not rip your clothes off and have you then and there, on the dance floor with everyone watching."

Journey swallowed, imagining it as vividly as if he really had done that. She could almost feel his strong hands lowering her to the ground, her clothes ripping like paper, the marble floor cold against her back, and Lucas kneeling over her, driving into her until she forgot about the onlookers and lost herself in him.

"Take me now," she said. "I'm yours."

He moved faster than she expected, sweeping her into his arms. She started to gasp with surprise, but it was cut off as his mouth came down on hers. His lips were soft and hot, and the inside of his mouth was like a furnace.

Of course, Journey thought dizzily. *He's a dragon. He can breathe fire.*

But the heat of his mouth was no more than the heat she felt building inside of her. She kissed him passionately, reveling in sheer sensation, in the touch of his tongue and the pressure of his fingers on her shoulders. But it wasn't just his touch that made her dizzy, it was *him*. He'd saved her life. He'd been wounded defending her. And he wanted *her*.

She could have kept kissing him forever, but Lucas stood up, lifting her as easily as if she was the tiny glass bottle of heartsease.

"You're so strong," she said, amazed. No one had ever lifted her before.

"I like the way you feel in my arms," he replied, pulling her tighter in to his chest.

In a few strides, he reached the huge bed and laid her down on the velvet cover. Journey stretched luxuriously, enjoying the softness of the velvet and the sight of Lucas, bare-chested, his dragonmarks gleaming, looking down at her with hunger in his golden eyes.

"What do you want?" he asked.

Journey hesitated. Even now, she found it hard to believe that a man—a prince—a dragon—would do what she asked, simply because she asked for it.

"Nothing?" Lucas inquired, with a teasing lilt in his voice. "There's absolutely nothing you want from me?"

Her doubts vanished. "There's a lot that I want from you. But you could start by taking off your clothes and letting me get a look at you."

"Your wish is my command," Lucas replied. Then his voice lowered, teasing gone, as he added, "I like that you want to see my body. I have been longing to see yours."

Journey swallowed. She'd never heard such naked, sincere lust in a man's voice before—never seen it in a man's eyes.

She lay back and watched as he removed his sword and hung it on the bedpost, then bent to take off his boots and breeches. The movement of his muscles beneath his skin and the glittering dragonmarks was almost unbearably sensual, as was the knowledge that this magnificent man was stripping for her pleasure. He pulled off his underwear, revealing a rampant erection pressing against his taut belly. Then he stood, letting her drink him in.

He hadn't taken off his jewelry. A heavy gold chain was clasped around the ivory column of his throat. More gold chains spiraled around his wrists and forearms. His long-fingered hands sparkled with gold and diamond rings. Journey wondered what all that gold would feel like against her skin, if it would be cool or warmed by the heat of his body.

Lucas turned slowly, letting her see every inch of him. The rippling muscles of his back. His fine ass. His long, lean legs, like a runner's. The glittering dragonmarks on his left shoulder extended a little way on to his back.

And then he turned to face her again. His eyes were like pools of molten gold. A pulse beat visibly at the fine skin of his throat. She could sense that he was barely holding himself in check.

"Do you like what you see?" Lucas asked.

"I do."

"Have you seen enough?"

"Lucas, I could look at you forever. But come touch me now." Journey beckoned him down.

He moved in a flash, kneeling over her before she could so much as blink. Now that he was closer, she could feel the heat of his body and smell his spicy scent. Before he did anything else, he leaned down and kissed her. The second kiss was just as thrilling as the first. Journey never wanted it to end.

But he moved downward, undressing her with his bejeweled hands as if he was unwrapping a precious gift. She shivered with excitement as he lifted her and loosened the ties of her corset. Her uncovered nipples hardened in the air, and he bent to kiss and lick each one. She gasped at the touch of his tongue, which sent ripples of flame through her body. All her senses were on fire.

As he moved downward, stripping off her dress and kissing every inch of skin as he slowly exposed it, she shuddered and writhed, instinctively trying to bring herself closer to his mouth. Every movement made the soft velvet of the bed cover stroke her body, caressing her back and ass and thighs. Lucas's chains slid smoothly along her skin. The contrast of the cool metal and the heat of his touch was almost more than she could bear. She heard herself making helpless little moans of pleasure. She couldn't remember ever sounding like that before, but she couldn't help it.

But before she could become self-conscious, Lucas lifted his head and said, "I love those moans of yours. Maybe later I can make you scream."

"I bet you can," Journey managed, before breaking off with a gasp as he flicked his tongue into her belly button.

Then he tossed aside her dress. He'd stripped her bare, and she lay naked and exposed before him. His gaze traveled hungrily over her body, and she could see in his expression that he found her infinitely beautiful and desirable.

"You're everything I've ever dreamed of," he said huskily.

Then he bent his head to taste her. His tongue was like a caress of fire, sending her nearly to the brink of orgasm with its very first touch. She grabbed the bed cover in both hands, clenching it in her fists, her back arching. Ribbons of flame licked at her clit and her sensitive inner walls until she felt like her entire body was on fire. She felt herself poised on the edge of climax for an endless moment, every cell of her body yearning for completion. And then she went over the edge in a white-hot burst of fulfillment.

Journey opened her eyes, which had fallen shut. "Did I scream?"

Lucas smiled like the cat that ate the canary. "Yes."

He began kissing and caressing his way back upwards. Journey had never come more than once while having sex, nor had she ever come just from having her body touched. But as Lucas slowly worked his way upwards, she began to think that she just might do both. Even his slightest touch sent ripples of pleasure through her nerves. She could tell by his loving attentions exactly how much he adored her and every inch of her body.

She didn't *quite* come from having her breasts kissed, though it was a near thing. Then he was poised atop her, his steel-hard cock pressed against her sensitive mound. He began to rub himself against her slick folds. Journey moaned as her clit swelled and throbbed. But she couldn't quite abandon herself to pleasure, forgetting all else.

"Wait," Journey said, though she hated to say anything that would make him stop, even for a moment. "I'm not on the pill—I haven't had sex in three years."

"I'll try hard to make up for that," Lucas replied. "But dragons do not have offspring easily. Unless I'm deliberately trying to make you pregnant, it can't happen."

Journey blinked. It sounded like such a line. Back in Lummox, guys were known to tell girls they couldn't get pregnant if it was their first time or they had sex in the shower or the man drank lots of Mountain Dew. "Seriously?"

"Seriously," Lucas assured her. "But if you're worried, we don't have to do anything that could even conceivably get you pregnant."

Journey looked into her heart, searching for any warning of danger, and found none. "That's all right. I trust you."

He again began to rock against her. She relaxed, giving herself completely over to passion. His rock-hard length rubbed against her clit, making her moan and cry out. It was so hard to keep her eyes open, but she loved looking at Lucas, at the gold of his eyes and hair and dragonmarks, at the sweat beading his forehead, at his muscular arms and shoulders. His chains had been warmed by her body, and now they felt hot against her skin.

Journey wrapped her arms around his back and held him tight as he pushed into her. She opened to him easily, loving the feeling of having his hard shaft inside of her. Every thrust stroked her clit, sending electric shivers through her body.

He moved faster and faster, harder and harder, pushing her down against the bed. She too felt hot and frantic. They kissed each other everywhere they could reach, her lips, his throat, her forehead, his cheeks. She tasted the salt of his sweat. His stubble was rough against her lips and skin. His spicy scent rose up, making her dizzy.

"Journey—" Lucas gasped. "My mate—*Mine*—"

He gave a hard thrust, sending her over the edge. Her climax shook her entire body. Journey heard herself cry out as she gave herself up to ecstasy. It seemed to go on and on, an exquisite moment stretching out forever. And then she descended from the heights like a dragon flying down to land.

"My dragon," she murmured. "I still can hardly believe this is real."

Lucas kissed her, his lips warm and gentle over hers. "I can hardly believe it either. And yet here we are. Together."

She buried her face in the crook of his neck, breathing in his spicy scent. His hair was smooth across her skin. As Journey fell asleep, she crossed her fingers that she wouldn't wake up and find that it had all been a dream.

CHAPTER SEVEN
Journey

Journey stretched and opened her eyes. A shaft of sunlight fell across the bed, making Lucas's hair and dragonmarks shine like the purest gold. He slept beside her, arms flung out and blankets tangled around his hips, his breathing steady and deep.

She watched him sleep, treasuring the intimacy of being able to do so. His eyelashes were long and golden, his full lips slightly parted. The long fingers of his left hand were curled around her wrist as if he didn't want to let go of her, even in sleep.

A wave of love and tenderness rose up in her, as powerful as the passion of the night before. He was a prince and a dragon, but also a man who had risked his life for her and let her see his pain. She couldn't imagine how any relationship between them could possibly work out, but neither could she imagine letting him go. Just the thought of it made her heart ache.

Lucas opened his eyes. He didn't seem surprised or alarmed to see her watching him, but smiled up at her as if she was the best possible sight to see upon waking.

"Good morning," he said, and pulled her down for a kiss.

Like every kiss they'd had, she never wanted it to end. She cuddled up close to him, luxuriating in the warmth of his skin against hers.

When their lips finally broke apart, she said, "I wish we could spend all day in bed."

"We could," Lucas replied. "That is, we could spend most of it. I need to go down to the kitchen and find some food. Flying takes a lot of energy. But I could come back and bring you breakfast in bed."

"A prince bringing me breakfast in bed," Journey said, laughing, and then sat up. "Never mind. I'll help you forage. Are you absolutely starved, or can we shower first?"

"Shower first," Lucas said decidedly.

She smiled to herself at his tone. Unlike other men she'd dated, Lucas obviously preferred to be meticulously clean. She bet she'd never have to remind him to put the toilet seat down.

In the bathroom, Lucas removed his bandages before stepping into the shower. Despite all the magic Journey had already seen, it was still astonishing to see how the raw wounds of the night before had healed into pink weals.

"Will they scar?" she asked.

"I doubt it. They weren't very deep."

She picked up his hand, loving that she could be so free with his body, and traced the little nicks and scars across his knuckles. "How deep were these?"

"Not very, but I got them over and over again. I think eventually my body got so used to them, it decided they were supposed to be there."

"But what are they from?"

"Bladework," Lucas replied. When Journey gave him a puzzled look, he elaborated. "Swordfighting, dagger fighting. I practiced every day since I was a boy."

"With weapons dipped in dragonfire."

"Sometimes," he said with a shrug. "And sometimes they were sharp."

Lucas turned on the shower, holding his hand under it to make sure it was warm before he beckoned her to step in. She wondered about his childhood and how normal he seemed to find it. He'd said it was stifling, but he'd never called it cruel. But whatever Lucas himself thought, if she ever met Grand Duke Vaclav again, she'd be tempted to punch him in the face.

She stepped in to the cascading water. The shampoo and soap smelled like Brandusan herbs, wild and spicy and astringent. Though Journey guessed that Lucas was too hungry for her to want to delay him, she did enjoy looking at his beautiful body glimmering under the sheen of flowing water. And she loved seeing how he looked at hers.

Obviously thinking the same thing she was, he said apologetically. "We can indulge ourselves here later. Or in the sunken tub."

"I vote for the tub," Journey said.

As she was toweling herself off, Lucas said, "Don't put on your old clothes. I'll find something clean for you."

"Clean freak," she teased.

"Better than a..." He paused, obviously searching for the phrase, and triumphantly said, "Better than a couch potato!"

Journey giggled. "That means someone who's lazy, not someone who's dirty."

"Oh, does it? I always pictured a man crusted with dirt, like a potato dug out of the ground."

"Nope. It's a guy who stays on the couch where you left him, same as if you'd dropped a potato there."

Lucas tapped her shoulder with an outstretched finger, wielding a mock sword. "I appoint you the royal slang coach."

Journey laughed as he strode off, a towel wrapped around his waist. He returned a few minutes later with an armful of clothing. "I raided the attic. I hope something will fit. For myself as well. I can't fit into anything I wore as a teenager."

As Journey put on a pretty blue skirt and blouse with stylized flames embroidered around the seams, she asked, "How much did you grow?"

"Six inches. All since I was eighteen."

"I'd have loved to have that happen that when I was that age," Journey said. "I really wanted to be slim and elegant."

"I hope you don't still." Lucas looked her up and down with open appreciation. "Your body is beautiful. Slim wouldn't suit you. And it's not pleasant to grow so quickly. It makes your bones hurt."

"It's all right. Now I like the body I have. And I love that you appreciate it!"

"Oh, I do." He ran his hand along the curves of her body, from shoulder to side to belly to ass, conveying his appreciation with his touch. Then, with visible reluctance, he pulled it away. "Let's get breakfast. Then I'll show you around."

He led her through more lavish corridors, decorated with gold and

71

marble, then into a distinctly less fancy kitchen. The refrigerator was empty, but there was a well-stocked freezer, pantry, and wine cellar.

"Do you cook?" Lucas asked.

"A little. What about you?"

"A little." He didn't sound very confident in his abilities. "I only learned when I left Brandusa. We have cooks in the palace, of course."

"Of course," Journey said, smiling. She couldn't imagine such a life. "I had a mom who cooked. She did try to teach me, but it never quite took."

"Perhaps we should not attempt anything difficult," Lucas said. "No soufflés, for instance."

"No strudel." Mrs. Florescu had demonstrated the art of strudel-making to Journey, culminating with a demonstration that perfectly rolled dough was thin enough to be pulled through a wedding ring.

Luckily, there was plenty of ready made and easy-to-cook food in the pantry and freezer. An American freezer would have been full of supermarket food, but the castle freezer was full of hand-wrapped packages with hand-written labels. Between the freezer and the pantry, they created a breakfast of pan-fried ham, toast with butter and plum jam, and coffee sweetened with wildflower honey. Lucas burned the toast, but Journey scraped off the black parts.

Lucas started to carry it all into the dining room, but both he and Journey hesitated at the enormous and intimidating table, with portraits of royal ancestors scowling down from the walls.

"We could eat in the bedroom," he suggested.

"What about outside?"

"Excellent idea." Lucas headed toward the doors. He had his hands full, so Journey went ahead, opening them for him, until they came to a garden.

The castle walls rose high around them, giving a sense of peace and privacy. They stood among a mock-wild abundance of trees and flowers. Bees buzzed around the roses and birds sang in the trees. A flock of pink and blue wild parakeets took flight when the door opened, chirping loudly.

Journey pointed to a tree with feathery leaves and sweet-smelling white flowers, shading a bed of thick green grass. "That looks like a good picnic spot."

"I expect it is," Lucas said. "But I know of a better one. Will you follow me into a labyrinth?"

A labyrinth! Journey thought delightedly.

"I'd follow you anywhere," she replied.

"Come, then." Lucas led her along the castle wall until they came to a wall of roses.

Journey shaded her eyes, looking up at it. She'd never seen such a tall hedge of rose bushes. It rose up ten feet tall or more, completely concealing whatever lay beyond it. It looked ancient, the twigs gnarled and heavy with dagger-like thorns. But it was lush with roses in every color: red, yellow, peach, pink, white, lavender, and a deep purple that was almost blue. The scent was intoxicating.

"It's like the briar roses guarding Sleeping Beauty's castle," she said. "Will we have to pick it apart twig by twig to get to the labyrinth?"

"It *is* the labyrinth."

Lucas led her further along the hedge as it curved around, until he came to an archway in it. Journey stepped through and found herself in a maze of rose hedges. The ground was thick with grass, and paths went in every direction.

"I hope I remember the way," he muttered. "It's been five years."

"If we get lost, at least we have provisions," said Journey.

He led her through the twisting paths, pausing now and then with a frown of concentration before he made his selection. Journey couldn't believe that she was being led through a labyrinth of roses by a dragon prince. It was like every dream she'd ever had, all come impossibly true at once.

Finally, they came to the center of the labyrinth. It was a glen carpeted in wildflowers, surrounded on all sides by red roses of every shade—scarlet, crimson, fire-engine, lipstick, burgundy, vermilion, swirled red and white, and a red so deep it appeared almost black.

Lucas set down his trays down, and they sat and had breakfast in the heart of the labyrinth. The air was warm and still, smelling of greenery, roses, and rain.

"How did you come to leave… Lummox?" he asked.

Journey couldn't help laughing at the disdain in his voice, which eased the sting of what she had to say in return. "After I graduated from high school, I was going to spend a couple years working and saving money, and then leave. So I worked the farms and imagined where I'd go. But before I could go, I met a man. His name was Scott Griffith, and he was a new farm hand in town. He was handsome and charming, and on our very first date, he told me he loved me."

"I see." There was an odd tone in Lucas's voice.

Journey was sure he was recalling the wild promises he'd made to her the first time they'd met. She still didn't know what to make of them. He *couldn't* have fallen in love with her at first sight—that didn't exist. Maybe he'd fallen in lust at first sight and liking at first conversation, and had mistaken it for love.

Unable to look into his eyes, she went on, "He seemed so different from the Lummox men. Romantic. Passionate. He promised me the moon and stars. He told me he'd love me forever and go with me anywhere I wanted. And I believed him."

Lucas's voice sounded dry and brittle. "I assume he was not to be trusted."

"No. He wasn't." Journey took a drink of coffee, but it didn't clear the lump in her throat. Why had she even started telling this story? She didn't want him to know how stupid and naïve she was. "One morning I woke up and he was gone. And so was all my money."

A low, menacing sound made Journey's head jerk up. Lucas's eyes had gone hot and bright, but not with desire. His cool exterior had given way to burning fury. "And where is this Scott Griffith now?"

"He doesn't exist," Journey replied. "It turned out to be a fake name—everything about him was fake. I have no idea who he even was, other than a con man. I found out later that he'd been going town to town, finding stupid girls like me and—"

"*No.*" Lucas laid his fingers across her lips, silencing her. "Never call yourself stupid. You were young and innocent. He took advantage of that. But you were not in the wrong to believe him. He was wrong to lie and steal and betray."

"I—" Her lips moved against his strong fingers. He dropped his hand, then tugged her close, cradling her against his chest. The contact brought tears to her eyes. "You're the first person to not blame me. Everyone in Lummox said it was my fault for being stupid enough to trust him. And they said if I'd spent my money on house payments like a normal person instead of saving it all, he wouldn't have been able to clean me out."

"And what did their normal person payments gain them?" Lucas asked rhetorically. "What a prize: a house in Lummox!"

Journey let out a watery giggle. "That's true. Well, I spent another two years working in Lummox, with everyone telling me every day that I'd never make it out—I'd throw my money away on the next handsome stranger to claim that he loved me. But I didn't. I bought a backpack and a plane ticket, and I left and never looked back."

"Never?" Lucas asked quietly.

Journey knew what he meant. She was forever marked by her past, just as he was. But she said lightly, "Almost never. I did see it in the news once, while I was in Budapest. It had been officially voted the most boring town in America. I felt totally vindicated."

Lucas's chuckle vibrated through his chest.

Journey settled back, leaning her head against his shoulder. "What about you? What have you been doing all these years away from Brandusa?"

He didn't reply. When she turned her head to see his face, she found him looking uncertain. He was biting his lower lip, a gesture she'd never seen from him before.

"If it's something you don't want to talk about…" Journey began.

"No. I mean…" His voice trailed off into silence.

"…then forget that I asked," she concluded.

"No, " Lucas said again. He hesitated again, then said, "I traveled. For years. I brought some of my hoard with me, so I didn't need to work. About a year ago, I was travelling in America. I was flying low at night over a city called Santa Martina. As a dragon, I mean. I was invisible, of course."

"Of course," echoed Journey, grinning.

"I saw a commotion in an alley, so I landed on a roof to get a better look. I saw a young man who looked like a gangster, covered in tattoos, fighting with an older man in a suit. The young man was trying to snatch the older man's briefcase."

"And you flew to the rescue?"

"Yes. I flew down to the street—the alley was too narrow for me to fit—became a man, and ran into the alley. I struck the man with tattoos and knocked him down, and handed the briefcase back to the older man."

"That's great!" But she saw from the ironic twist in his mouth that the story wasn't going to be as straightforward as she'd thought.

"The tattooed man jumped up and tackled me," Lucas went on. "We began fighting. I realized immediately that he was a shifter too—he was far stronger than any human could be. We were struggling together, and then he shouted, 'Roll!' I don't know why I didn't think it was a trick, but I didn't. We both rolled to the side, and a bullet struck where we had been. The man with the briefcase was firing a gun at us—at both of us."

"But you'd rescued him," Journey said, perplexed.

"I too was confused," Lucas admitted. "I let go of the tattooed man and tried to disarm the man with the gun. So did the tattooed man. The gun was knocked across the alley. Then the man who had been shooting at us became a leopard and jumped for the tattooed man's throat."

"What!"

"And the tattooed man became a wolf." Lucas seemed to be enjoying Journey's surprise. "By then I had no idea who was the hero and who was the villain. I wasn't sure who I should help, so I tried to get between them and stop them from killing each other. Then I heard sirens. Both the shifters turned back into men. The police arrived, along with a very big man in plain clothes. The police arrested the man with the briefcase. He had been conducting industrial espionage, and the briefcase contained stolen documents. I told the police I had seen fighting and had tried to intervene. Of course I didn't mention the shifting."

"So what was going on?" Journey asked, fascinated. "Was the werewolf an undercover cop?"

"No, he was private security. Once the police were gone, he turned to the big man and said—excuse the profanity—'That motherfucking wannabe hero's a shifter! He's the one who broke my fucking nose!' And then he explained what had happened, in similarly colorful language."

Journey giggled as Lucas went on, "And the big man offered his hand to me, and said, 'I'm Hal Brennan, and this is Nick Mackenzie. I run an all-shifter private security company called Protection, Inc. Are you looking for a job, by any chance?'"

"And you took it?" Journey asked.

"I hadn't intended to. But the wolf shifter said, 'You're not going to put that arrogant prick on the team!' I didn't like his tone. So I couldn't resist taunting him by asking Hal to tell me more about the job. The more he said, the more intriguing it sounded." Lucas shrugged. "I suppose I was tired of traveling and wanted a rest. I thought I'd try it for a month or two. But I've—I *had* been working at Protection, Inc. for six months. It was… difficult to leave."

"So you're a *bodyguard?*" Journey asked, delighted.

"We do other jobs as well. But yes."

"It suits you." Journey once again saw him placing his body between her and six assassins, his sword gleaming in the moonlight. "Do you like it better than being a prince?"

"Yes." Lucas wrapped his arms close around her. "And most of all, I would like to protect *you.*"

"Why do *I* need protection?" It had been nagging at her mind all along. "I'm a nobody—just another backpacker. But you said at the river that those assassins were after *me.*"

"Because…" Lucas took a deep breath. The sunlight glittered in his topaz eyes. "Journey, this may be hard for you to believe."

"Harder than dragons?"

"Perhaps." His serious tone made her stomach clench nervously. "Raluca and I swore a vow of honor to marry. Our marriage would seal treaties between her country and mine. If we do not marry, those treaties will be void. Many people stand to gain power or wealth by those treaties, and so have a strong vested interest in our marriage."

Journey couldn't imagine what it would be like to have her most personal choices have such huge repercussions. "If I knew that any date I went on might affect my entire country, I'd probably never date at all. Except *that* would affect my country too. You must be under so much pressure."

Lucas was silent for a moment, his gaze lowered. When he spoke, his voice was lower, rougher, as if he'd started to choke up. "You're the first person who's ever cared about that."

He cleared his throat and went on, "However, I have a way out. The agreement said that if Raluca or I found our mate, the arrangement is off."

"What's a mate?" Journey asked.

Lucas's voice dropped again, but this time she could hear that it was from passion. "My mate is the love of my life. She's the woman I saw across a crowded room, and knew she was meant for me. Journey—it's you. You're my mate. You're the woman I'll love and protect forever, if you'll have me."

She looked deep into his amber eyes, and saw nothing but sincerity and love. Journey's heart felt filled to the brim with joy, hot and sweet as dragonfire. She was too moved to speak.

He went on, "I know you've been lied to before. I don't know how to convince you that I'm not another charming con man. I—"

"No!" Journey twisted around in his arms until she was sitting on his lap and facing him. She cupped his face in her hands, feeling the strong lines of his jaw and the rough stubble coming up on his cheeks. "Lucas, I know you're honest and honorable and everything you say you are. I love you too. I think I loved you from the first moment I saw you. I just thought love at first sight was one of those impossible things that I was stupid to believe in."

"Like dragons?"

"Like dragons." She tugged his collar aside to trace the pattern of his dragonmarks.

Lucas reached out to her. His rings glittered in the sun as if he held fire in his hands. Then he put his palms on the back of her head and drew her into him.

At the first touch of his lips to hers, Journey's blood caught fire. The sensual coziness she'd felt nestled in his arms transmuted to shockingly intense desire. She gasped into his mouth, her heart accelerating as if he'd lit a quick-burning fuse inside her. She didn't want to lazily snuggle and kiss, she wanted him to rip her clothes off and take her.

She could feel his heart pounding as well. His hands dropped from her head and clenched on her shoulders, fingers sinking into her soft flesh. She couldn't tell if what she felt was pleasure or pain, but she liked it. When she opened her eyes, she was unsurprised to find that his were brilliant gold.

"Now, Lucas," Journey gasped. "I want you in me, now!"

He lowered her to the ground in an instant. The sudden drop gave her a brief thrill of danger, as if she was falling. But he cradled her in his arms for a gentle landing. For a moment he was still and poised above her as she lay on her back, his gaze hungry, the sun bright on his hair. Then he was shoving up her skirt, his hands clumsy with urgency.

There was a flurry of hasty fumbling; they were both too intent on getting to each other to care about careful undressing. Journey yanked at Lucas's shirt and ripped it open. Pearl buttons popped off and scattered all around. Lucas jerked her panties down and left them halfway down her thighs, too impatient to take them all the way off. When he reached down to his breeches, his hands were actually shaking with desire. She had to help him undo the ties.

"Come on," she heard herself muttering, without having any intent to speak. She felt out of control in the very best way. "Come on, Lucas! Come on!"

The knot finally gave way, freeing his rock-hard shaft. He dropped down on top of her and plunged himself into her. Journey cried out in ecstasy. The moment of penetration was so satisfying, it was almost an orgasm in itself. He filled her completely, his cock hard and hot inside of her.

She lifted herself up to meet him, frantic with desire, her hands slipping over his sweat-slick skin. The scent of grass and roses and arousal dizzied her. He kissed her hard as he thrust, each movement taking her closer to the brink. She could tell that it wouldn't be long for either of them. His heart beat like a drum against her chest.

He gave a final hard thrust, and jerked back his head to call out her name. His brilliant eyes opened wide as he reached his own climax. And then Journey came in a burst of fulfillment, only a heartbeat behind Lucas, overcome by ecstasy and love.

He rolled off her and lay beside her on the soft grass. They were both breathing hard, their hearts still pounding. Then they relaxed into the afterglow. Lucas reached upward, stripped the petals from a scarlet rose, and scattered them over Journey's body. They fell lightly on her sensitized skin, like drops of sweet-smelling, crimson rain.

"Rubies on pearl," Lucas said softly. "You are a treasure."

"I can hardly believe that this is real," Journey said. "I thought I'd never love a man again. I thought I'd never *trust* a man again. And I sure never thought anyone would fall in love with me—especially not someone as cool as you!"

"Oh, am I cool now?" Lucas inquired, smiling. "Nick once called me the opposite of cool."

"What does he know? He's probably still mad because you broke his nose."

"Perhaps." Lucas sat up, then earnestly bent over her. "There is one last thing I haven't told you. I didn't want you to feel pressured. But I don't want to lie by omission, either. Also, it involves your safety."

"What is it?" she asked, alarmed.

"The arrangement between myself and Raluca..." Lucas began.

I knew it, Journey thought with an inward sigh. Royalty might seem romantic and glamorous, but she was beginning to wish Lucas was just a bodyguard with no other entanglements.

He went on, "The only way for me to break it is for you to appear in court and declare your intention to marry me. You have one month to decide."

Much as she loved him, that instinctively put her back up. She didn't like being bossed around and pushed into a commitment, especially one with a deadline. "Says who?"

"The ancient traditions of dragonkind," Lucas replied glumly. "Backed up by the royal families and parliaments of Brandusa and Viorel."

"Yikes." Hastily, Journey added, "It's not that I don't want to marry you. I love you! I'm sure I *would* like to marry you some day, but it's so soon to get engaged. And I don't like being bossed around. I especially don't like being strong-armed into a lifelong commitment on an arbitrary deadline. Lucas, do *you* want to get engaged this soon?"

His handsome face creased in a frown. "I would if I wasn't being forced into it. And if I wasn't forcing you."

"You're not forcing me. Your government is." Once she'd heard her own words, the whole idea sounded even worse. "You know what, that settles it. I don't want the government setting the date for our engagement. We should get engaged on a date *we* choose."

"I feel the same way. That's why I haven't proposed to you. I want to wait until you have a free choice. And, of course, until I have obtained a ring worthy of your finger." He lifted her hand and kissed it.

Any one of Lucas's rings could probably purchase an entire farm in Lummox. Her mind reeled at the thought of what he'd consider worthy. "So how do we get out of it? Do you just tell them all to shove it?"

Thoughtfully, Lucas said, "Do you know, I once thought that I could never do such a thing. It would be breaking a vow of honor. But now that I've met you, I see that there is more to honor than keeping agreements dreamed up by others for the sake of profit and politics. There is also the honor of the heart."

"So you'll tell them to shove it?"

"I'll tell them to shove it." But his smile didn't reach his eyes. "But there is something else I need to attend to. As I said, a number of people will benefit if Raluca and I marry. I believe those assassins were sent to kill you by someone who wants to make sure I marry Raluca. I am not sure that person will give up so easily. I need to find out who they are."

"Any ideas?"

"It could be Raluca's uncle, Duke Constantine. He would gain profit and power through the treaties with Brandusa. Or... I don't like to believe this, but it might be my great-uncle, Grand Duke Vaclav. He may believe that he still influences me as he did when I was young, and wish to be the power behind the throne."

Journey had seen that expression of cool ruthlessness on Lucas's face before, when he had stood between her and the assassins. "Should we go back to the palace and investigate?"

"*I* will go back and investigate," Lucas replied. "You'll be safer here. No one knows where you are."

"Isn't your spare castle kind of an obvious place to look?"

He smiled. "We have many spare castles. But don't worry. Dragons have a special bond with their mates. It's how I knew you were in danger on the riverbank. If you're in danger, I'll know. And I'll come flying to save you."

"But—" Journey began.

"But what if I cannot come all the way from the city in time?" he interrupted. "Then go to the castle caretakers—they have cottages in the woods outside the walls—and they will hide you."

"Thanks," Journey said. "But that's not what I was thinking. What if *you're* in danger?"

Lucas seemed startled by this question. "Oh—Well—Journey, I *am* a dragon. And also a bodyguard. Danger is quite literally my business. You mustn't worry about me. I am quite capable of protecting myself."

"I know." His argument was reasonable, but she still felt uneasy. "How long do you think you'll be gone?"

"No more than two days. If I'm not back by this time, two days hence…" In the carefully controlled voice he used when he was trying hard to suppress some emotion, he said, "Go to the caretakers and tell them you need to be smuggled out of the country, immediately."

Journey's heart lurched. "Lucas, if you don't come back, I'll go looking for you!"

"No!" His unexpected shout made her jump. More calmly, he said, "I swear to you, I will come back. But it is not easy to imprison a dragon. If I do not return…"

"You're dead," she said flatly.

"If I do not return, there will be nothing you can do to help me." He bent and kissed her eyelids; her eyes had begun to brim with tears. "Do not think on it. It *will not* happen."

Journey fought to control her emotions. She hated the thought of Lucas going alone into danger, and wished she could at least go with him.

Stupid small-town girl, she told herself fiercely. *Who do you think you are? You're not a magical shapeshifter. You're not a warrior princess, like you used to imagine. You're just a chubby little backpacker. If he did get in trouble, you being there would only make it worse—he'd be distracted trying to protect you.*

Journey made herself smile. She didn't want him distracted by worrying about her, either. "I trust you. And I know you'll come back for me."

CHAPTER EIGHT
Lucas

Lucas hated to leave Journey, but he couldn't justify deliberately taking her into danger. He led her out of the labyrinth, and then they stood in the garden, kissing and holding each other, neither willing to let go.

Finally, he forced himself to step away. "I will be back soon."

Journey gave him a shaky smile. He didn't know whether to be glad that she cared enough to worry about him or sad that she was worried. "I know you're a brilliant swordfighter and a bodyguard and a dragon. But... Be careful."

"I will not take foolish or reckless action," Lucas assured her. "At Protection, Inc., Nick and Destiny considered me to be overly cautious."

That seemed to reassure her. She gave him one last, lingering kiss. "Go solve the mystery. I know you can do it."

He stepped away from her and the nearest trees, and allowed his mind to fill with a dragon's longings. He would fly high, he would burn his enemies to ash and gone, he would find the finest treasure in the land and lay it at his mate's feet.

His blood ran hot and his wings unfurled. Lucas leaped upward into the sky. Below, Journey waved him on, her expression bright with unspoiled joy in watching his transformation. He dipped a wing in response, then concentrated to make himself invisible to all but other dragon shifters. He hoped Journey would enjoy the surprise of watching him blink out of view. Then he flew on, leaving the castle behind.

The forest spread out below him. Now and then he glimpsed a cottage or a castle. The trees grew less dense as he came closer to the city, broken up by large glens and shining lakes. When he had been a young dragon, he had learned to dive into the lakes and snatch fish in his jaws, like an osprey. Lucas dipped lower, thinking to do so now. Transformation took a great deal of energy, and he was very hungry.

A burning pain pierced his chest. Then a second, agonizing shock wrenched at his body, forcing it to change shape against his will. He was suddenly a man again—a man falling from the sky.

Dragonsbane! Lucas realized. *I've been shot with an arrow dipped in dragonsbane!*

He hit the water with bruising force and plummeted toward the bottom. He instinctively held his breath and tried to swim away under-water. But his chest burned with pain, and he was dazed from the fall and the shock of the icy water. His boots and sword were pulling him down, forcing him to exert himself just to keep from sinking further.

He barely made it to the shoreline before he was forced to surface. He managed one gulp of air, and then rough hands seized him.

It was a group of masked men, like the assassins who had tried to kill Journey. Lucas fought, but he was outnumbered and wounded and breathless. Before he could do more than knock one man down, some-thing sharp stung his back.

More dragonsbane, he thought, wincing at the idea. But though the pain didn't increase, he immediately felt dizzy.

No, he realized. *It's a tranquilizer.*

Lucas woke abruptly, his eyes flying open and his body jerking. Metal rattled. He was standing up, cold stone at his back and cold metal around his wrists and ankles. Even without looking, he knew the metal wasn't gold.

There was no moment of disorientation. He immediately remem-bered what had happened. And with a single glance, he knew where he was.

He was chained to the wall of one of his own family's dungeons.

It was a small cell of gray stone, smelling of dust and granite. There were no windows, but burning torches cast a flickering light.

84

Lucas jerked at the chains, but they had been made to withstand even the more-than-human strength of shifters; his ancestors had sometimes imprisoned each other, usually in battles over the throne. He pulled and yanked as hard as he could, but accomplished nothing more than making his wrists and ankles bleed.

He finally gave up and leaned against the wall, exhausted. He still wore his jewelry, but his sword was gone. The wound in his chest seemed shallow and small, no more than a pinprick—it must have been a dart rather than an arrow—but it felt like a red-hot poker had stabbed him through and through. His dragon was silent within him, quelled by the dragonsbane still burning in his veins.

But his physical pain and helplessness concerned him less than the implications of his plight. Whoever had imprisoned him obviously didn't want him dead, so his jailers couldn't be after the throne itself. They were most likely the same people behind the attempt on Journey's life.

In that case, he was imprisoned to stop him from protecting her. They probably meant to keep him here while they searched for her. Once they found and killed her, he would be released.

Lucas knew it was useless to struggle, but a surge of fear and rage made him again throw himself against the chains. A red haze clouded his sight. He felt no pain. He heard himself shouting, but he didn't know what he was saying. He could think of nothing but protecting his mate.

Cold water dashed into his face, bringing him to his senses. Lucas coughed and shook his head, blinking to clear his vision.

A masked man stood in front of him, holding an empty bucket.

"Fight as hard as you please," the man said coldly. "It won't change a thing."

Lucas didn't recognize his voice, other than that his captor had a Brandusan accent. Then he looked closer and saw that the man wore an earbud. He must be getting his orders from someone trying to conceal his identity. Every word he said was probably dictated by an unseen watcher.

His knees felt shaky and every muscle in his body ached, but Lucas took a deep breath and made sure his voice was calm.

"No matter what, I will not marry Raluca. If you kill Journey—"

The thought of it choked him. It was so easy to picture her sprawled on the ground, her emerald eyes glazed in death, her warm heart stilled forever. When he went on, he despised himself for being unable to prevent his voice from shaking. "If you kill her, I still won't marry Raluca. So there is no point to any of this. Drug me again and release me. I don't know who you are, so I won't be able to take revenge."

There was a pause, no doubt while the watcher spoke into the earbud. Then the masked man said, "I do not believe that you would betray the honor of a lineage of a thousand years for mere revenge."

"Believe it," Lucas said.

Another pause. "Princess Raluca knows nothing of this."

Lucas had never thought she did. But suspicious of where the conversation was going, he didn't reply.

"If you will not marry her, she is worthless," the masked man continued. "Then I will have to kill her *and* you. That will leave one of your cousins to inherit. And then I can arrange an alliance for that cousin which will suit me almost as well."

Lucas stared at the masked man, letting his dragon show in his eyes. The man took an involuntary step back.

As I guessed, Lucas thought. *He's not a dragon himself. He's just some trusted minion.*

"Release me." Without even meaning it, Lucas heard his voice drop to a draconic hiss. "Do you know what it means to imprison a dragon? Do you know what it means to threaten a dragon's mate? Dragons do not forget. Dragons do not forgive. If by some miracle you live to escape this cell, I will hunt you to the ends of the earth. Nothing you have been promised is worth dying in dragonflame."

Once again, the man took a step back. Then he jumped as if someone had shouted in his ear. Squaring his shoulders, he demanded, "Where is Journey Jacobson?"

Fury burned within Lucas, but he restrained himself from struggling. Thrashing around and exhausting himself would get him nowhere. But even chained and unable to shift, he had his voice and his wits.

A dragon's tongue is sharper than a dragon's tooth, spoke the sweet remembered voice of his mother.

His father had added, *Do not forget, Lucas. Words are weapons.*

"Heed my promise," Lucas said. "I speak to both of you, the man who stands before me and the man who whispers in his ear. If at any time you release me and leave Journey unharmed, I swear on my honor that I will not take revenge. If you harm Journey or do not release me of your own accord, remember my other promise. Dragonsbane has an antidote. I will not be a man forever."

The masked man twitched nervously. He took a step toward Lucas, then another. His head darted this way and that. Then he suddenly thrust his hand into his pocket, bringing out a key.

"You will not regret this," Lucas promised.

The cell door was flung open, and four more masked men burst in. One grabbed the man holding the key and hustled him out. The other two grabbed Lucas and pinned him tight to the wall, while the third shoved a gag into his mouth.

Lucas was ready to explode with frustration. He'd been so close to escape!

"Your tongue is as deadly as your flame," remarked the man who had gagged him. "You may not speak except to tell us where Journey is. When you're ready to do that, tap your right hand against the wall."

Lucas closed his right hand into a fist.

The man who had spoken reached into his pocket and removed a vial. "Have you ever swallowed dragonsbane?"

Only pride saved Lucas from letting the nauseating rush of fear show on his face. That was supposed to be the most agonizing form of torture in existence. They said that dragons who were subjected to it begged for death.

"Where is Journey?" the man demanded.

Lucas tried to think quickly and clearly, for he suspected that soon he would not be able to think at all. His family had ten castles scattered across the country, most in areas unreachable by motor vehicles. It would take a dragon days to search them all, and it would take weeks for his minions to do so. Unless Journey was very unlucky and they chose to search her castle first, all Lucas needed to do to signal her to flee was to hold out for two days.

Two days of hell, he thought. *Can I bear it?*

He opened his hand and tapped the wall. When the man undid his gag, Lucas said, "I flew her to the airport in Budapest. She's halfway to America by now. I was going to renounce the throne and follow her there, but first I wanted to find out who had tried to have her killed."

It seemed like a plausible story. It certainly would have been a better choice than what he'd actually done.

The masked man slapped him hard across the face, snapping his neck back and knocking his head into the wall. "Liar."

"It's true!" Lucas protested. "Don't you think I'd do anything to keep her safe?"

"I know dragons and their mates. You wouldn't have been able to bear parting from her so quickly. Where is she?"

Stubbornly, Lucas repeated, "She's on an airplane."

"Pry his jaws open."

Lucas fought, but there was little he could do with his arms and legs bound. The men dug their thumbs into his jaw, forcing it open, and grabbed a handful of his hair to jerk his head back. Then his chief captor stepped forward and poured a stream of dragonsbane down his throat.

It burned like acid. Lucas tried to spit it out, but the men forced his jaws together and pinched his nose shut. In his struggle to breathe, he swallowed involuntarily.

The pain was like nothing he'd ever felt before. He'd thought the dragonsbane would burn his throat and stomach, but the agony only started there. Within seconds, it spread through his entire body. Lucas tried to double over, but the manacles held him tight.

Don't scream, he thought desperately. *Don't give them the satisfaction.*

A minute later, he was screaming.

"I tire of listening to him," the masked man said. "Gag him again."

Lucas barely noticed as the men again stuffed the gag into his mouth. He could feel nothing but agony burning him alive from the inside out. He understood now why victims begged for death.

I can't bear it, he thought. *I would rather die than endure days of this.*

But then he thought of Journey. She loved him. It would break her heart if she lost him. For Journey, he had to hold on.

For Journey, he thought to himself.

He clung to her name like a spar as he was tossed about in a sea of pain.

For Journey...

For Journey...
For Journey...

The pain stopped.

At first Lucas couldn't comprehend what had happened. Then he tasted the sharp tang of heartsease. They must have poured some into his mouth. He tried to lick his lips, and found that he could. The gag had been removed.

It was another minute or so before he recovered enough to open his eyes. He was dangling from the manacles, his clothes and hair drenched in sweat. His whole body was shaking uncontrollably.

The masked man leaned forward, vial in hand. Lucas flinched back, but all the man did was flick a single burning drop of dragonsbane on to Lucas's hand.

Of course. They still needed to prevent him from shifting. Lucas wished he'd thought of it as soon as he'd come to, then realized resignedly that he wouldn't have had the strength to shift anyway. Even without the dragonsbane, he doubted he was strong enough now.

"That was twenty minutes," said the masked man.

Lucas stared at him, disbelieving. Surely it had been hours!

He's lying, Lucas told himself. *He's trying to scare you.*

It was working. Whether it had been hours or minutes, Lucas knew he couldn't endure that agony again.

"Where is Journey Jacobson?" the man demanded.

Now that the dragonsbane no longer burned within him, Lucas could register the cramping pain in his shoulders and wrists. He attempted to stand up, but his legs wouldn't support him.

"Talk," said his captor.

Lucas tried, but his throat was too raw and dry. He got one syllable out, then broke into a fit of painful coughing.

His captor reached into a bag and brought out a flask. Lucas flinched again as the man raised it to his lips, but the liquid inside was only water. He was allowed a few swallows before it was withdrawn.

"Talk," the masked man repeated.

"Castle Balaur." Lucas had to force the words out. They felt as if they choked him.

The man stood still, staring at him. He—or rather, his hidden master—was no doubt trying to tell if Lucas was lying.

Whoever captured me knows me well, Lucas thought. *Even if it's only by reputation and a few brief encounters. They know about mates, and how much I must love Journey. They know of my honor and they know of my pride. And they know I would not give her up unless I was broken beyond repair. I have to prove that they broke me.*

An idea came to him immediately, but his pride made him hesitate. Then he thought of Journey, of her open heart and her courage, and reminded himself that he would do *anything* to protect her.

He focused on his pain. On his fear for himself. On his fear for Journey. On his regret at leaving his friends at Protection, Inc. without so much as a proper goodbye. On his stupidity at getting himself captured. On every humiliation he'd suffered at Grand Duke Vaclav's hands when he'd been a boy. And instead of keeping his feelings under control, he invited them to sweep him away like a dry leaf in a hurricane.

Deliberately, he thought, *If Journey dies, it will be all my fault.*

Lucas began to cry. Hot tears ran down his face as sobs racked his body.

Even as he let himself drown in terror and despair, a cool, distant part of him thought, *It's been twelve years since the last time I cried. I'd forgotten how it makes your nose run.*

He'd been eleven and sparring with Grand Duke Vaclav, bare-chested and with blunt swords dipped in dragonsbane. His great-uncle had "killed" him repeatedly and criticized his technique at every blow. After an hour of that, Lucas had begun to cry, more from humiliation than from pain.

His great-uncle had said, "Those tears do more to prove you unworthy of your name than any amount of poor technique. Dragons do not weep, so you must not be a true dragon. I doubt that you will ever be able to transform."

Lucas spent the next two years terrified that he really would be one of those rare, tragic people who were born into dragon families but never managed to shift. And he had never wept again.

Now, in that cool, distant part of his mind, he wondered if Grand Duke Vaclav was the watching mastermind. He hoped so. His great-uncle would find a tearful breakdown very convincing.

For a moment, Lucas thought his ploy had worked. Then the

masked man slapped him across the face.

The blow was nothing, given the pain he was already in. It was the knowledge of what it meant that made his heart sink.

"Liar," his captor snapped. "We already searched Castle Balaur."

"Then she's already fled." But Lucas knew they could hear the lie in his voice.

The masked man picked up the bottle of dragonsbane.

In his entire life, Lucas had never known such dread. His heart felt like a lump of ice in his chest. But now that he had no further use for tears, they stopped as if he'd turned off a tap.

Lucas closed his eyes. For Journey, he would endure.

CHAPTER NINE
Journey

Journey watched Lucas soar into the sky, his scales the gold of sunlight against the deep blue sky, until he vanished between one blink and the next.

She lay on her back on the grass, looking up into the sky. After the dullness of her first twenty-two years, her life had become such a rollercoaster. Europe. Brandusa. Assassins. Dragons. Lucas. She'd gotten everything she'd ever dreamed of and more. And if she lost it—if she lost *him*—her heart would break and never mend.

"He's a *dragon*," she said aloud, trying to convince herself. "He'll be perfectly safe. If anyone tries to hurt him, he can bite their head off or stab them with his sword or punch them and break their nose."

She wasn't normally a violent person, but the thought consoled her. She just wanted Lucas to return safe and sound.

Journey lay for a while in the sun, thinking of Lucas and watching butterflies flit about the garden. She was so still that a huge butterfly with a black body and shocking pink wings landed on her chest. It rested there a while, while she hardly dared to breathe, and then flew off to resume its quest for nectar.

She stood up with a sigh, gathered up the breakfast tray, and headed back for the kitchen. Since she had no other way to make herself useful, at least she'd wash the dishes.

Help Lucas!

The breakfast tray fell from her hands. Journey spun around, looking for the source of the voice. But no one was there.

Lucas needs you!

This time she recognized the voice as coming from within her, not from outside. It was her own thought, but so urgent and fierce that she hadn't recognized it at first.

Go! Journey's inner voice shouted. *Go now!*

Her heart was pounding, and her breath came fast. She felt as she had on the riverbank, when her gut had told her she was in danger. And her gut had been right.

That way!

But this was more than simple instinct. Journey not only knew that Lucas was in danger, she knew how to find him. She was drawn toward him like iron to a magnet: *that way.*

She didn't doubt it for an instant. Lucas had already told her that because they were mates, he'd know if she was in danger. He hadn't mentioned it working both ways—maybe Lucas himself hadn't known that it could—but obviously it did.

Journey started to bolt *that way,* then stopped. All she knew was that he was in terrible danger and which way she needed to go. Her inner voice said nothing about what the danger was or how far away Lucas was. She had no idea what was going on or what she'd need to help him. And if there was one thing she'd learned as a backpacker, it was that if you were going to walk into a place you didn't know much about, you'd better be prepared.

It almost killed her to turn her back on the call, but she made herself run into the castle rather than out the gates. Her shoes clattered over the marble floors as she dashed up the stairs. Lucas had gone to an attic to find women's clothes, and she'd need to hide her incredibly non-Brandusan hair if she wanted to leave the castle without immediately being spotted by assassins.

To her relief, the attic wasn't hard to find. She opened wooden chests until she found a green headscarf, like Brandusan woman often wore while doing housework, and tied it tightly around her head. Then she hunted until she found a sturdy leather backpack stashed at the bottom of a closet.

Journey checked herself in a mirror. With her hair concealed, she looked like any Brandusan woman. Thank goodness she was curvy.

She'd fit right in.

Go! The voice shouted, making her jump. *Go now!*

"In a minute!" Journey said aloud.

She ran down to the bedroom and swept a medical kit into the backpack, started to run out again, and then remembered that the assassins had used dragonsbane on Lucas. She ran back in, grabbed the bottle of heartsease, and stuffed it into her skirt pocket.

Lucas is in danger!

"As if I don't know," she muttered.

Finally, Journey ran to the kitchen and flung dried fruit and several canteens of water into her pack.

Go—The voice began, then shut up as Journey hurried out the door. Once she was headed in the right direction, it seemed satisfied.

She went out the front gates and let her inner magnet lead her in the right direction. That turned out to be cutting straight through the woods, following what she'd seen of Lucas's flight path.

She tried not to worry so much that she couldn't think straight, but it was hard not to. What if she arrived too late? What if she arrived in time but couldn't help him? What could a completely ordinary woman with no special skills do to rescue Lucas, when being a brilliant fighter and a dragon shifter hadn't been enough to save himself?

Journey hurried through the woods, glad that if nothing else, she was at least used to hiking long distances. Maybe once she got to wherever he was, she could whack his enemies with the backpack.

She hiked all morning without a stop, occasionally drinking water and eating a handful of dried fruit as she walked. At mid-day, the inner voice, which had shut up for the entire hike, suddenly yelled, *Here!*

Journey jumped in surprise, then snuck forward until she could peek through the trees. *Here* was a castle nestled in the woods, similar to the one Lucas had left her at, but without a wall around it. No one was in sight.

Any suggestions? Journey inquired of her inner voice.

It was silent. If Lucas was in there, and presumably he was, he must be locked up. There was no sound of fighting or shouting or anything at all. The silence was eerie.

Since she didn't have any better ideas, she snuck around to the back. With any luck, it would have a servant's entrance. If anyone caught her, she could always claim to be a caretaker.

Journey's heart pounded as she approached the small wooden door at the back of the castle. To her relief, it opened, though with a creak that made her nerves jitter. No one was in sight. She walked inside, stepping softly to prevent her shoes from clattering over the marble floor.

I wish I was a shapeshifter, she thought. *I wish I was a bodyguard. If I get out of this alive, I'm at least going to take a martial arts class.*

But though she had no training, she did have her wits. If Lucas was imprisoned here, the logical place would be the dungeon. Dungeons were underground. So she was looking for stairs down or a trap door. Hopefully, not the same stairs that his jailers were using.

Prisoners needed to be fed. If there was a separate servants' entrance, it would probably be near the kitchen. Using the layout of Lucas's castle as a rough guide, she searched until she found a kitchen. That had no trapdoors or stairs going down, so she opened the pantry door.

Here! Her inner voice shrieked.

Very helpful, Journey told it. She'd already spotted the door half-hidden behind a cupboard, carved with unnerving scenes of torture and imprisonment.

She had to unload everything out of the cupboard before it was light enough for her to move aside without making any telltale scraping sounds. Then she opened the door to a flight of stone steps leading down into darkness.

Journey began to tiptoe down the stairs. Soon she was in total darkness, forced to feel her way down. She expected to be stabbed in the back by assassins or grabbed around the ankle by a monster at any second. Sweat ran down her back, though the air was cool.

Then she took another turn and saw flickering orange light. Journey froze, listening. She could hear a man's harsh breathing, but nothing else.

Here!

The steps led to a dungeon lined with barred stone cells, all empty. She crept forward until she came to the source of the light, a cell lit by burning torches.

Lucas was chained to the wall.

Journey pressed her knuckles hard into her mouth to stifle a gasp.

He was unconscious, his head hanging down and his arms stretched up above him. She didn't see any blood, but he was drenched in sweat and breathing as if pain had followed him even into sleep.

She tugged at the cell door, careful not to rattle it. The door was locked.

"Lucas," she whispered.

He didn't stir.

She whispered louder. "Lucas! It's Journey!"

That didn't wake him either, and she was afraid to speak louder. Whoever had locked him up had to be nearby.

She wanted to rip her hair out with frustration. He was hurt and in terrible danger, but though she was only six feet away from him, she couldn't get to him or help him. She couldn't even let him know she was there without endangering them both.

Journey forced herself to think. There had to be *something* she could do.

She could leave, find a telephone, and call the police. But she hated to abandon Lucas, let alone for the hours—maybe days—that would take. He could be dead by the time anyone got there.

Journey looked around the dungeon, hoping for a stray iron bar she could use to bash someone over the head. She didn't see one, but she did notice a small wooden table with a vial full of clear liquid, placed right outside Lucas's cell. That was odd.

She glanced back into the cell, then at the table. It would be directly in his line of sight if he'd been awake. If that was deliberate, then he was supposed to look at that vial. It must have been left there to intimidate him when he woke up.

Poison? Journey thought, then guessed, *Dragonsbane.*

Then she heard footsteps coming down the stairs at the other end of the dungeon. She had no time to wonder if she was right. Moving as fast as she could, she opened the vial, dumped the liquid into her backpack so it wouldn't make a telltale stain on the ground, yanked the bottle of heartsease from her pocket, poured it into the vial, capped the vial, and replaced it on the table.

By the time she was done with that, the footsteps were almost at the dungeon. Terror vibrated down every nerve as she fled for the servants' stairs, trying to move as fast as she could without making a sound.

She could hear voices by the time she reached the stairs. Journey darted upward until she was in darkness, then sank down on the hard stone steps, her pulse thundering in her ears.

She could see nothing, but she could hear everything. Footsteps. The cell door rattling open. A hard slap. A muffled groan, quickly cut off, that pierced her to the heart.

And then a voice she didn't recognize. "Where is Journey Jacobson?"

"That's the wrong question." Lucas's voice was hoarse and stressed, but his crisp intonations were unmistakable. "You should be asking, '*Who* is Journey Jacobson?'"

"Play games with me, and I'll have you gagged again," snapped the other man.

Lucas went on as if the man hadn't spoken. "Journey Jacobson is my mate. She's the woman I love and always will. It is my honor to protect her to my dying breath."

Journey's heart ached to hear Lucas's words. Even tortured and chained and threatened, with no idea that she was there to hear him, his thoughts were on her. That was what she'd always imagined love to be—always secretly believed love to be—though everyone told her fairytales weren't real, happily ever afters didn't exist, and love was no deeper bond than mere shared interests and sexual attraction.

If the heartsease didn't work, Journey would run down the steps and fight to save the man she loved. She couldn't imagine that having any outcome other than getting herself killed. But she had to try. She couldn't leave Lucas to die alone.

Another slap echoed against the stone walls. Journey winced in sympathetic pain.

The other man spoke loudly. "You'll change your tune soon enough. Pry his mouth open."

CHAPTER TEN
Lucas

Lucas fought the men holding him, but he had little strength left. They easily forced his head back and pried his jaws apart. Even that brief struggle left him dizzy, his heart fluttering unevenly in his chest.

I won't have to endure this for two days, he thought. *A couple more doses, and my heart will give out.*

Maybe one more dose will do it.

Some people might welcome death as a release from suffering, but Lucas didn't. Instead, he was filled with bitter regrets. He'd saved Journey, but he'd never get to have a life with her. He'd never work again with the crew at Protection, Inc. Raluca would be murdered or forced into another unwilling marriage. He'd never have a chance to stand up to Grand Duke Vaclav. He'd never touch gold again or weigh a diamond in his hand. He'd never dance with Journey again or travel with her to the places she loved best.

His entire body tensed as the liquid hit his throat. But it didn't hurt. Surprised, he swallowed automatically. And tasted the familiar tang of heartsease.

How in the world…?

Then his practiced instincts took over. If he'd learned one thing at Protection, Inc., it was that a missed opportunity might never come again. He didn't waste time wondering how or why, but focused on using this chance before it was gone.

As soon as the men released him, he closed his eyes and slumped in the chains as if he'd passed out again. Cold water splashed into his face, but he didn't stir. His attention was turned inward, seeking his dragon.

Despite the heartsease, the aftereffects of the poison lingered. Lucas felt dizzy and sick, his breathing labored, his heartbeat weak. His arms and shoulders burned with pain, and his bones ached with cold. It was hard to focus on anything but how terrible he felt.

Lucas had never tried to shift when he was this exhausted and ill. Nor had he ever shifted in a space too small for his dragon. He didn't know whether he would break the cell walls or crush himself to death. But it was his only chance.

For Journey, he thought.

And then, surprising himself, *For me. I want to live. And I want to have a life. If I make it out of here, I swear on my honor that I'll tell the entire royal family to shove it.*

The thought gave him strength. Lucas reached as deeply into himself as he ever had, and found a lust for gold, a love for flight, and a longing for freedom that surpassed all else.

He found his dragon.

His blood blazed with a fire that didn't hurt. He opened his eyes and saw his captors scrambling backwards.

"Duke Constantine!" shouted the masked man. "He's shifting!"

The three men bolted out of the cell, leaving the door open, and fled for the stairs.

His vision was hazed by a whirlwind of golden sparks. Lucas gloried in it. His wrists and ankles grew, snapping the manacles. The walls of the cell collapsed as his body expanded.

Protect Journey!

Simultaneous with his dragon's roar, he heard Journey's voice. "Lucas!"

Lucas stared. Impossibly, Journey was running toward him. Blocks of stone were falling from the ceiling. One smashed to the floor right in front of her, making her leap to the side with a scream.

His heart nearly stopped, but it was too late to turn back the change. Lucas lunged forward, spreading out his wings over his mate. He caught her up and pulled her close to him, sheltering her with his body as the entire castle came down on top of them with an earsplitting crash.

When the dust settled, Lucas found himself half-buried in rubble. His first thought was for Journey, but he could feel her breathing, huddled against his chest and covered by his wings.

He was bruised all over and he could feel small trickles of blood running down his body, but he didn't seem to have any serious injuries. His dragon's bones were strong yet flexible, and his dragon's hide was very tough. He carefully rocked himself back and forth to dislodge the worst of rubble without dropping it on Journey, then scooped her up and sprang aloft.

The fresh air and sunlight were a delight beyond measure after that endless time in the dungeon. He recognized the surroundings as those of Castle Abur, another family retreat. The castle itself was a ruin. Lucas landed, carefully depositing Journey on the grass, and became a man again. To his immense relief, she was completely unhurt—not even scratched.

She threw her arms around him, tears gleaming in her eyes, and gave him the sweetest kiss he'd ever known. "I was so afraid for you."

"I was afraid for *you*," Lucas replied. "How did you get here?"

"I knew you were in danger." After a beat, she added, "I walked."

He couldn't help smiling. The simple answer to the complicated question: that was so Journey. He could get the details later. For now, he was filled with a Journey-like uncomplicated happiness that he was alive, she was alive, and she was with him.

"Duke Constantine imprisoned me and forced me to swallow dragonsbane," Lucas said. "He was trying to make me to tell him where you were. But just now one of his men accidentally gave me the antidote instead of the poison. Isn't that absurd? I would not have believed such a mistake could happen if I read about it in a book."

"That's because it wasn't a mistake," Journey replied. "I found you in the cell, but I couldn't get you out. I couldn't even wake you up. But they had that bottle of dragonsbane outside to scare you if you came to. So I dumped it out and replaced it with heartsease."

Lucas's heart was warmed with love and admiration. "How clever of you! So you were the one who saved me."

Journey indicated the ruined castle. "I just helped you save yourself."

"As I said," returned Lucas.

Journey followed him at a distance as he inspected the rubble. He found four masked men unconscious within it and pulled them out, laying them on the grass. He took off their masks, but didn't recognize any of them. They must be hired criminals.

Lucas heard the tiniest rustle behind him. He spun around. Sunlight gleamed on Duke Constantine's sword.

Lucas leaped aside. With no time to summon the concentration necessary to shift again, he snatched up a stone and hurled it at his enemy. Duke Constantine ducked. Lucas tensed, uncertain whether to put his body between the duke and Journey, or to try to lure the duke away from her.

But Duke Constantine ignored Journey, though he had to have seen her, and lunged forward. Lucas barely managed to sidestep the strike, then scrambled backward. The duke was obviously planning to kill Lucas first and then go after Journey. He clearly didn't consider her a threat.

Out of the corner of Lucas's eye, he saw Journey scrabble in her backpack, then pull out a blanket. Lucas tried not to look at her lest he tip off the duke. He guessed that she'd try throwing it over his enemy's head.

Good idea, Journey, he thought. He could use all the help he could get.

Duke Constantine closed in on him, slicing his sword at Lucas's head. Lucas was again forced to jump aside. He threw another rock, but the duke dodged it easily.

Journey came up behind him and swung the blanket like a whip. The end caught the duke across the face. Duke Constantine yelped in pain. Taking advantage of his distraction, Lucas lunged forward, caught the duke's wrist, and twisted it to force him to drop his sword. Before his enemy could recover, Lucas threw him to the ground, drove his knee into the small of his back, and pinned his wrists above his head.

"Good work, Journey," Lucas called. "Now give me the blanket. I'll tear it up and bind his wrists."

"I don't think you want to touch it," Journey replied. "It's where I dumped the dragonsbane."

Lucas laughed. No wonder the duke hadn't shifted after Lucas had disarmed him! He tore up Duke Constantine's own shirt to tie his wrists behind his back.

His prisoner lay in still and furious silence. Lucas was content with that. He had no desire to talk to him. Lucas used the other criminals' shirts to bind them hand and foot, for they would undoubtedly regain consciousness before the police could arrive.

"Would you like to ride on dragonback again?" Lucas asked Journey.

"Yes, of course." She beckoned him out of the duke's earshot and put her arm around him. "You don't look good. You're bruised and bleeding and you're white as paper. And you feel cold. *Can* you fly?"

The adrenaline high of battle still tingled in his veins, giving him a strength that he knew wouldn't last long. "I can fly long enough to make it back to the palace. We can't stay here. I need to get you to safety and him to justice."

"What about you?"

"I need to get myself to bed. I am very tired."

Journey grabbed his wrist. "Lucas, you need to get yourself to a hospital. You told me dragonsbane is a poison!"

"I took the antidote."

"Yeah? And how do you feel now?"

"Not good," he admitted. "But I cannot have been given a fatal dose, or I would already be dead."

Lucas knew there was some flaw in his logic that Grand Duke Vaclav would have immediately pounced on, had he been present. But he was having trouble focusing on anything but getting back to the palace, disposing of Duke Constantine, and making his mate less frightened. She had gone so pale that her freckles stood out like drops of blood.

"There are doctors at the palace," he added belatedly.

That seemed to reassure her a little. "Okay, good. Let's go to the palace."

He thought of gold and flight and vengeance, and became a dragon. Journey climbed on his back, and he scooped up the duke in his talons. Then he took flight, barely skimming above the treetops, too tired to climb higher. Lucas didn't make any special effort to ensure that the highest leaves and twigs smacked Duke Constantine across the face, but he didn't make any special effort to avoid it, either.

After what felt like hours of weary flying, first the city and then the palace came into view. Lucas landed on the palace roof and dumped the duke unceremoniously to the ground. Then he became a man and yanked his prisoner to his feet.

Lucas marched Duke Constantine down the steps leading into the palace, Journey following beside him. To Lucas's relief, the duke had apparently decided it was undignified to struggle and didn't put up a fight.

The adrenaline rush had worn off, leaving Lucas dizzy and exhausted. His throat and chest and belly burned, his bones ached, and he felt chilled and feverish by turns. His heart kept stuttering off-rhythm. Breathing hurt. Swallowing hurt. Everything hurt. All he wanted to do was lie down. He'd feel better once he slept.

You just have to get through the next half hour or so, he told himself. *That's all. You can do it.*

He didn't feel like he could get through one more minute.

Both his hands were occupied with the duke, but Journey put a gentle hand on his back. "How are you feeling?"

Lucas jerked his head at Duke Constantine, trying to convey that he couldn't confess to weakness in front of his enemy.

"Right." Journey said no more, but kept her hand where it was. It was a small touch, but it comforted him. Her love and support gave him the strength to go on.

At the doors of the throne room, the guards stared at him, then the duke, then Journey, then back to him.

"Your highness..." A guard ventured at last. "Shall I summon a doctor?"

"Not now," said Lucas. Speaking hurt, too. "I will see one later."

"*Yes,*" said Journey. "Summon one right now! Tell the doctor he was forced to swallow dragonsbane."

Lucas was touched by her concern. "Very well. Have the doctor wait outside the throne room. Also, please dispatch the police to Castle Abur. They will find four criminals tied up near the rubble. They should be arrested and held on charges of assault and kidnapping."

"Rubble?" asked a guard.

Journey jumped in. "And tell the doctor he had a castle collapse on top of him! Though that was when he was a dragon."

The guards stared.

"Open the doors," Lucas commanded.

The guards obeyed. It was late in the day, most of the ordinary business done. No petitioners were present. The throne room was occupied only by King Andrei, Queen Livia, Grand Duke Vaclav, Princess Raluca, several of Lucas's cousins, and a handful of courtiers and guards.

If Lucas had any lingering suspicions of his great-uncle, they were put to rest by Grand Duke Vaclav's sincerely bewildered stare. Lucas scanned everyone else's faces, just in case, but not one of them betrayed anything but surprise, confusion, and concern.

"Duke Constantine attempted to murder my mate," Lucas began, then briefly recounted the entire story.

Everyone listened in shocked silence. But as soon as Lucas concluded, Duke Constantine drew himself up to his full height and blustered, "This is all a pack of lies. The prince has gone mad!"

Journey's glare could have cut diamonds. "I saw the entire thing. Every word Lucas says is true."

Duke Constantine shot her a contemptuous look that made Lucas want to slap him, then turned back to the onlookers. "Would you take the word of an American tourist against the word of a duke? But your majesties, Princess Raluca cannot marry a madman. Nor can a madman inherit the throne. Prince Lucas must be stripped of his title, and the marriage agreement and all its associated treaties must be transferred to your eldest son."

Before Lucas could say a word, Raluca stood up and marched across the marble floor. She wore the traditional wooden heels, and every step was loud as a gunshot.

Raluca stopped in front of Duke Constantine. Each word rang out with cutting clarity, like shards of broken crystal. "You are a liar, a traitor, and a criminal. And I am not your property."

"Of course you are not." The duke spoke with a false kindness that made Lucas's skin crawl. "But it is your duty as a dragon and a princess to marry to benefit your country."

"I am tired of being used," said Raluca. "I want to be more than a pawn in someone else's game."

"You are no pawn. Some day you will be a queen." Duke Constantine's tone was halfway between a promise and a threat.

Raluca stepped forward, encroaching on the duke's personal space. Lucas noticed for the first time that she was taller than her uncle. "I am tired of being any sort of game piece. I wish to have a life of my own, independent of politics."

Duke Constantine glared at her, puffing out his chest as if to make up for his lack of height. "Don't be childish. Royalty can never be independent of politics."

"I know." Raluca held her ground, pale but defiant. "And that is why I renounce my title and my claim to the crown."

"What! You can't—"

"I do." Raluca's precise tones cut him off more effectively than if she'd shouted. Turning away from him, she said, "Lucas, we may not meet again, but I will always consider you my friend. Be well. I wish you the best of lives. King Andrei, Queen Livia, thank you for your kindness. Farewell."

"What do you mean, farewell?" Duke Constantine demanded. "Where do you think you're going?"

"I'm free now." Her face lit up with an amazed smile, as if she was marveling at her own reply. "I could go anywhere at all."

She whirled around and ran for the balcony, her silver hair streaming behind her. Journey started forward with a gasp, but Lucas caught her arm.

"She's a dragon," he reminded her. "She doesn't fall. She flies."

Raluca threw herself over the railing. The woman dropped out of sight. A moment later, a silver dragon soared up. The sun gleamed on her wings as she flew upward and away, farther and farther into the blue until she became a glittering point like a daylight star. And then she was gone.

"She can't do that!" Duke Constantine shouted belatedly.

Journey turned on him. "She just did, asshole. And good for her!"

Lucas wanted to laugh, but he'd suddenly gotten very dizzy. Black spots floated across his field of vision. He bit down hard on the inside of his mouth, hoping a small shock of pain would help him focus.

The spots faded, but the dizziness remained. The king and queen were conversing with each other, their voices too low for Lucas to catch the words, but their whispers sounded unnaturally shrill in his ears.

King Andrei snapped his fingers. "Guards! Take Duke Constantine to the dungeons."

The guards hauled the duke away. He protested all the way, until the heavy doors closed behind him and cut off his voice.

Lucas spoke hastily, while he still had a chance. Despite the burning pain in his throat, his voice rang out loud and clear. "King Andrei, Queen Livia, I too renounce my title. I renounce my claim to the throne in favor of whichever of your children you choose to name as your heir. From now on, my life and my love are my own."

"You can't do that!" Grand Duke Vaclav shouted.

He sounded so exactly like Duke Constantine that Lucas did laugh. That was his downfall. The room began to spin around him, going faster and faster until he lost his footing.

"Look to the prince!" a voice called out.

The next thing he knew, someone was trying to pour liquid into his mouth. Lucas lashed out, but a hard grip caught his hand. He struggled, jerking his head to the side and clenching his jaws.

Soft hands stroked his hair. "Lucas, it's all right. It's medicine—it won't hurt you."

His vision cleared. He was lying on the floor of the throne room with his head in Journey's lap. One of the royal doctors was attending to him. The guards and courtiers were gone, but the royal family sat in a semi-circle around him. Grand Duke Vaclav had an iron grip on his wrist.

Lucas wrenched his arm free. "Don't touch me."

"I was only trying to help," his great-uncle said stiffly.

"I don't want your help." Lucas took a deep breath, then another, willing himself to calm. His mind cleared, allowing him to focus on the doctor. "I will take the medicine now."

The doctor shot Lucas a nervous glance. Lucas couldn't blame him. If Grand Duke Vaclav hadn't stopped him, Lucas probably would have punched the doctor in the face.

"Here, give it to me." Journey took the cup from the doctor's hands, lifted Lucas's head, and held it to his lips.

He swallowed the medicine. The familiar tang reassured him. It was heartsease, but a far larger dose than he'd ever taken before.

"We will speak again when you are well," said Grand Duke Vaclav. There was an ominous note in his voice.

"We will not," replied Lucas.

With a flash of anger, his great-uncle said, "You have no idea what I wish to say to you!"

"Even now, you are trying to bully me while I'm lying here ill," Lucas pointed out. "You have had my entire life to speak to me. I know what sort of words you have to say, and I do not wish to hear them. I am not giving you an order as your prince. I am telling you, man-to-man, to *go away*."

His great-uncle stared at him. Lucas met his cold gaze without flinching. Then Grand Duke Vaclav stood up and walked away without another word. The heavy doors of the throne room closed behind him with a very final-sounding thud.

"Good for you." Journey spoke for his ears only.

Despite the heartsease, dizziness again closed in on him. Lucas had hoped to finish his business, walk to his room, and *then* collapse, but he resigned himself to being carried out on a stretcher.

"Journey is my mate," he said, hoping his voice would be heard. "Extend her every courtesy."

Queen Livia squeezed his hand. "Of course we will. Lucas, please relax. Nothing will harm her or you."

"*I* can give a grand duke orders," King Andrei added. "Vaclav will be going on a restful vacation in the countryside until you return to America. You will not see him again."

Lucas did relax upon hearing those promises. The last thing he felt was the gentle touch of Journey's fingers in his hair.

CHAPTER ELEVEN
Journey

Lucas was carried to his bedroom on a stretcher. The doctor, the king and queen, and Journey followed, and stayed after the stretcher-bearers were dismissed. Lucas lay unconscious in his canopied bed, his face white as his pillow. Even after he'd taken the heartsease, he was cold to the touch. His breathing was barely perceptible.

Journey stood by the bed, her heart squeezed painfully in her chest. Lucas couldn't die now, after enduring so much. He *couldn't*.

She was terrified that he would.

Journey was not reassured when the doctor pulled an ancient, witchy-looking book out of his bag and consulted it, muttering that there hadn't been a case of dragonsbane poisoning in a hundred years. Then he woke Lucas.

"How much dragonsbane did you swallow?" asked the doctor.

It took Lucas a moment to answer. He seemed to find it difficult to speak. "Two or three…"

"Two or three drops?" the doctor asked, looking relieved. "Good. I had worried that it was more. You will be better in a few—"

"Two or three *spoonfuls*," Lucas corrected him. "Five times."

Terror washed over Journey at the expression on the doctor's face. Finally, he said, "Are you certain?"

Lucas nodded.

The doctor stared at him, then turned away and picked up the witchy book again. While he was consulting it, the king stepped forward.

"I shall pour the same dose down Constantine's throat," said King Andrei.

Lucas shook his head.

"Andrei, no," said Queen Livia. "That has been banned in Brandusa for a hundred years. It would be dishonorable to break our own laws for the sake of personal vengeance. Let us use only a touch of dragonsbane on his skin, just enough to keep him from shifting. And let us imprison him for life in our darkest, deepest cell, so he may never again know the freedom of the skies."

The king looked at Lucas. "Would that content you?"

Lucas nodded.

"Very well. He may suffer more from that in the long run." King Andrei sounded as if he hoped the duke would.

The doctor closed the book and poured out another cup of heartsease, looked at Lucas, then handed it to Journey.

"I am not going to strike you," Lucas said to the doctor, with the faintest touch of exasperation.

Journey sat on the edge of the bed and held the cup to his lips. Lucas drank, then closed his eyes. Silence fell. She touched his cheek, but he didn't stir. Despite the roaring fire in the hearth and the blankets piled over him, he was still very cold.

"Will he be all right?" Journey blurted out. She'd been biting her lip before, too afraid to ask.

"It's hopeful that he's lived this long," replied the doctor evasively. "He is very strong, or he would have died in the dungeon."

"He is a dragon," added the king. "We are hard to kill."

Lucas's eyes fluttered open, and he took Journey's hand in icy fingers. "I won't leave you, Journey. I swear it on my honor."

She blinked back tears as she said, "I'll hold you to that."

The king and queen kept the promise they had made in the throne room. They treated Journey with courtesy, never questioned her relationship with Lucas, and had a smaller bed moved into his room so she could stay by his side.

The doctor came several times a day, each time consulting his witchy book as if he hoped something new had been written in it when he wasn't looking. When Journey peeked over his shoulder, she read what she had already guessed: the dose Lucas had been given should have killed him outright, and heartsease was the only real treatment.

Other than that, it said that patients should be kept warm and well-nourished. If they survived long enough, the dragonsbane would eventually work its way out of their bodies. It concluded by saying that most victims of small doses lived and most victims of large doses died. After she read that part, Journey wished she hadn't looked.

The poison affected Lucas's throat, making him unable to swallow any solid food. Though the palace cooks provided everything from broth to milkshakes, he lost weight at an alarming rate. And though he never complained when he was awake, he often cried out in pain in his sleep.

Sometimes Lucas was weak but clear-headed. He couldn't speak easily, so Journey would sit by his side and tell him stories about her travels. Sometimes he slipped into delirium, shouting hoarsely that he'd been shot and calling on his friends at Protection, Inc. for backup. Journey was sure that if he was in his right mind, he wouldn't want her to tell him any lies, however comforting. But she had to say something. She settled on telling him that his friends would do whatever they could to help him. That had to be true, and he always relaxed when he heard it.

Journey too did whatever she could to help him, talking to him, rubbing his back, stroking his hair, and holding him in her arms. When he was dazed or delirious, he wouldn't allow anyone but her to give him anything to drink. It made her wonder how deeply he'd been scarred, entirely apart from the physical damage, by his time in the dungeon. She felt utterly helpless. But her touch seemed to comfort him, and he knew her even when he recognized no one else.

King Andrei and Queen Livia visited Lucas often. Journey suspected them of feeling guilty over sticking him with the arranged marriage and letting Grand Duke Vaclav bully him when he was a boy, but she said nothing about that. They were certainly kind to him now.

Better late than never, she thought.

Once when Lucas was having a bad night, tossing to and fro and muttering that he was burning and freezing, Queen Livia left, then returned with a gold nugget as big as her open hand.

"From my own hoard," she said to Journey, as if that was an

explanation.

The queen pressed it into his hand. Lucas clutched it to his chest, then curled into it, relaxed, and went to sleep.

"I'll have to let him keep it now." The queen sounded as if she regretted it already. "It's difficult—painful, even—for dragons to give up gold once they've slept on it."

Definitely guilty, Journey thought. But it fascinated her to learn more about dragons. She realized now why the doctor had only pushed Lucas's jewelry around when he'd cleaned his wounds, rather than attempting to remove it.

"I've noticed that you don't wear jewelry," Queen Livia remarked. "I hope you don't dislike it. He'll want to give you some once he's better."

"I love jewelry," Journey replied. "I've just never been able to afford the good stuff, and I don't like plastic."

The queen glanced at the glint of gold showing through Lucas's fingers. "I don't think that will be a problem."

One morning Journey woke to find Lucas's bed empty and the shower running. She sat bolt upright, her heart lifting. It was the first time since been poisoned that he'd been strong enough to do more than walk the few paces to and from the bathroom, leaning heavily on someone's arm.

The sound of the shower stopped. A few minutes later, the bathroom door opened. Lucas stepped out, his hair wet and his gold chains gleaming, walking by himself for the first time in a week.

"Lucas," Journey began. Her voice caught, and she was unable to go on.

"I was tired of sponge baths," he said.

She ran up and threw her arms around him. He bent down and kissed her. His lips were hot again, the touch of his skin like a midsummer day. She hadn't cried once in the entire time he'd been so ill. She'd wanted to be strong for him. But as if his heat had melted something in her, she abruptly dissolved into a flood of tears. He held her tight, standing steady as a pillar of steel, while she sobbed on his shoulder.

"I was so afraid you'd die," she gasped. "And it was because of me.

You let yourself be poisoned to protect me. I wish it had been me instead."

"Journey…" Lucas stroked her back and shoulders. "You must not feel guilty about that. I am glad it happened as it did. If it had been you who had come so close to death, I could not have borne it. I think this time has been harder for you than it has been for me."

Journey wiped her face, trying to get control of herself. "I don't know about *that*."

"I have the benefit of not recalling much of it," Lucas admitted, then hastily added, "And you needn't recount it for me. From what I do remember, I would be embarrassed. Though I am very curious how I seem to have acquired the prize nugget from my aunt's hoard."

"You were in pain and you couldn't sleep," Journey said. "She gave it to you to make you feel better."

Lucas stared at her. "Dragons don't do that. A small item, perhaps. A diamond they are not fond of. But not their best gold nugget!"

"I think she felt guilty over mistreating you when you were a boy."

He still looked baffled. "She never mistreated me."

"She let your great-uncle be cruel to you."

"None of us thought of it as cruelty at the time." Lucas's gaze strayed to his bed, where a glint of gold was visible from under the pillow. "Well, that was very kind of her. It's an exceptionally fine nugget."

"Are you going to give it back?" Journey inquired mischievously.

He looked appalled. "I *slept* on it."

Journey laughed.

After that, Lucas recovered quickly. Once he could eat again, the palace cooks sent a non-stop stream of delicacies to his room, and he rapidly regained the weight he had lost. Soon he was walking around the palace, and then the gardens, and finally the city.

Journey took him to meet the Florescus, who were delighted to see Journey again—and be visited by a prince.

"Come see me in America," Journey suggested.

"In Lummox?" Stefania asked doubtfully.

Lucas shook his head. "In Santa Martina. It's a big city in California, between San Francisco and Los Angeles. I have an apartment there."

"Oooh," Stefania squealed. "And Journey will be sharing it!"

"That's right." It was one of the things she and Lucas had decided while he'd been recovering.

"Can I go?" Stefania started to turn to her parents, then exclaimed, "Ha! I'm an adult now! I don't need to ask. I'll take my backpack by myself, just like Journey. And Doru will go with me!"

Her mother smiled. "Of course you may go to America. But you needn't take a backpack."

"Now that those awful treaties with Viorel have been cancelled, I'm not worried about money," Mr. Florescu added. "We can all visit America!"

After they left the Florescus, Lucas said thoughtfully, "I wish I'd paid more attention to what ordinary people thought of those treaties. I was so convinced that it would sully my honor to break the engagement, I didn't give any thought as to whether it would even be good for Brandusa. I suppose it goes to show that I never was meant to be a king."

Journey put her arm around his waist. "Looking forward to going home?"

"Yes. Very much. But before we go, I want to get you something."

He strode along the cobblestones, making her hurry to keep up. His body was once again hot against hers, his stride energetic, his amber eyes bright and clear.

She was beyond glad that he was well again. And she'd never forget that he'd willingly endured agony to protect her.

Lucas escorted her into the fanciest jewelry shop in the city. Journey had seen it before and even wistfully stared into the windows, but had never had the nerve to go inside. It looked like the sort of place that wouldn't welcome broke backpackers.

"Pr—Er—Welcome!" The jeweler stammered, obviously uncertain what to call Lucas. "May I show you something?"

Everyone who encountered Lucas had that awkward moment. Brandusan royalty had no surnames. (To Journey's amusement, he had told her that a confused DMV person had issued his American driver's license to "Lucas Blank.") Prince Lucas was no longer correct, but Lucas by itself was far too intimate for strangers. In Brandusa, only friends and relatives addressed each other by their first names alone.

"We would like to see everything," Lucas replied. "Please open the cases."

As they began to inspect the jewelry, Journey suggested, "You should give yourself a surname. What about Gold?"

Lucas shook his head. "Too American. It would feel false."

"I know what you mean," Journey replied. "I'm never going to like Lummox, but it's still a part of me. If I'd grown up somewhere more interesting, maybe I wouldn't have been in such a hurry to get out and see the world."

"I could be Dragomir, perhaps," Lucas said, after a moment. "I believe I have some long-lost distant relatives of that name."

"I like that."

He lifted a necklace from the case in front of her. "This? Or the name?"

"Both." She ran her fingers over the pendant dangling from a delicate gold chain. It was small but beautifully detailed, depicting a dragon in flight. Now that she had seen dragons, she knew it was also completely accurate.

"Choose as many pieces as you wish," Lucas said. "You should have something to wear for all occasions. But I would like you to have one that you wear always. Like a wedding ring. But it needn't be a ring. It could be any shape, so long as it's gold."

The more she looked at the pendant, the more she liked it. "Would this do?"

"Perfectly." Lucas took it from her hand and pressed it to his lips. Then he lifted her hair to clasp it around her neck. It was still warm from his touch, and settled into the hollow of her throat as if it had been made for her.

They selected several more pieces: a wrap-around gold chain bracelet similar to his but with smaller links, a pair of teardrop emerald earrings, an elegant choker of diamonds and aquamarines, a silver ring shaped like a fish holding a pearl in its mouth, and an exquisite star sapphire ring. But her favorite was the dragon pendant that meant as much to Lucas as a wedding ring.

"Enough," she said at last. "I won't be able to walk!"

"You needn't wear them all at once," Lucas replied, though she was certain he would like it if she did. Gold and jewels meant far more to a dragon than their monetary worth.

"You can buy me more in America," she suggested.

That promise extracted him from the shop. Outside, she stood in the sunlight wearing the jewelry he'd bought her, enjoying his heated gaze on her.

"I could wear it all to bed," she suggested. "And nothing else."

"Yes," Lucas said, his voice lowering to a purr. "You should do that."

They returned to the castle and said their farewells. Lucas packed his hoard, possessively fingering the queen's gold nugget before he tucked it away and tied the pouch around his waist. Journey hefted her old backpack, which she'd retrieved from the Florescus' home.

On her way out, she caught sight of herself in the mirror and laughed. "A king's ransom in gold and jewels, and a beat-up backpack that's been rained on in half the countries in Europe."

"Cherish that backpack," said Lucas. "It's been a good friend to you."

"It has." As they walked up the stairs, she asked, "Is there anything like that for you? I mean, other than your hoard?"

"While I was at Protection, Inc., I did become attached to my car and my gun." Lucas frowned. "Unfortunately, I gave them away. It would be ungentlemanly to attempt to take them back. I could buy new ones, but…"

He'd told her the story of his break with Protection, Inc. and how bad he felt about it, and confessed that he didn't know how they'd react when he returned.

"But that particular car and gun were special," she finished. "You know, Lucas, I think you're worrying too much about those guys. It sounded to me like they were pissed off because they care about you and you were shutting them out."

"Perhaps." He sounded doubtful.

On the roof, she watched him become a dragon. Like the necklace he'd given her or Lucas himself, it was something that never ceased to bring her joy. When the sparks faded, she climbed on his back and they launched into the blue.

The trip took several days, for they stopped to spend the night in hotels in various countries. Though they'd never gotten engaged, much less married, Journey felt like they were on their honeymoon.

At last they flew into Santa Martina. Journey had never been there before, and it had been a year since she'd been anywhere in America.

She wondered if she'd settle in as if she'd never left or if she'd feel like a foreign traveler in her own country.

Lucas landed on a rooftop. Journey slid off and watched him transform in a whirlwind of gold.

"Is this your apartment?" she asked doubtfully. It was in a business district and looked like an office building.

"No, it's—" Lucas broke off. "My apologies. I was thinking of going home. It seems my dragon had his own idea about where that was. This is Protection, Inc. I could fly you to my apartment now, though. I'm sure you'd prefer to shower and change your clothes before you see anyone."

Journey nudged him in the ribs. "You mean, *you'd* prefer to shower and change."

And put off seeing them, she thought. Though he appeared as cool and collected as ever, she knew how tense he had to be.

His amber gaze met hers, and she knew that he had guessed her thought. "Then come meet my team."

He led her down a flight of stairs and into a sleek lobby. Journey set her backpack on the floor and went to get a better look at the framed photos on the walls. They were all of wild animals—a grizzly bear, a snow leopard, a wolf, a tiger, a panther, a pride of lions, and...

"It's you!" She pointed to a photo of the palace at Brandusa, the white marble bathed in a sunlit glow, with a golden dragon circling overhead.

Lucas was eyeing it as if he'd never seen it before. "Hal never took it down. I told him I wouldn't come back. I never called to say otherwise. But I'm still here with the rest of the team."

A deep voice rumbled behind them, "That's because you *are* part of the team."

"You idiot," a woman's voice added.

Journey turned to see a tall, burly man with hazel eyes and a short, curvy black woman standing in the doorway. She recognized them from Lucas's descriptions as Hal Brennan, the leader of Protection, Inc., and Destiny Ford. More people crowded in behind them.

"What've you been *doing* all this time?" demanded a young man with tattooed arms and intense green eyes. He had to be Nick Mackenzie, the guy whose nose Lucas had broken. When she looked closely, she could see a tiny bump on its bridge.

"I've been teaching a horse to fly," Lucas replied.

Nick stared at him. "What the fuck does that mean?"

Journey almost jumped out of her skin when a tall man with black hair and ice-blue eyes appeared beside Lucas. She'd somehow failed to notice him in the crowd. He handed Lucas a gold-plated gun. "Best pistol I've ever fired. Thanks for the loan."

An elegant blonde woman snatched the gun from Lucas's hands. "I don't think so, Shane. Lucas left without saying good-bye. He doesn't deserve nice things like Desert Eagles."

"I let Fiona borrow it," Shane informed Lucas. "She liked it too. Now you'll never get it back."

Destiny put her hands on her hips. "I'm definitely not giving back the Porsche Carrera. That's your punishment for disappearing on us!"

A handsome Latino man remarked, "I don't mind returning your apartment, but I don't know if you'll want it back. I've completely re-decorated. I put a mirror on the ceiling over the bed... Installed a hot tub... Hung some red velvet drapes for atmosphere... Oh, and the bed vibrates now. But you might like that."

Lucas looked briefly horrified, then laughed. "I'll have it all de-livered to your apartment, Rafa. Shall I throw in a box of extra-small condoms?"

Rafa put on an exaggeratedly wounded look. Destiny licked her finger, then snatched it back. "Burn!"

Hal strode forward and clapped Lucas on the back. "Welcome home."

Lucas's eyes shone, but with a clear light rather than a hot one. Journey had never seen him cry, but she suspected that he was hold-ing back tears. When he spoke, his voice was suspiciously choked-up. "Thank you, Hal. Everyone... I am sorry about how I left. And I am glad to be back."

Everyone immediately began talking amongst themselves. Journey could see they were giving Lucas space to recover his composure. She appreciated that right up to the point where they started talking to her.

"Hey, Red. Are you that fucking foreign princess he had to marry?" Nick demanded.

"Nope," Journey said. "I'm a backpacker from Lummox."

"Where the fuck is Lummox?"

"It's in the middle of fucking nowhere, North Dakota," Journey replied. "And by the way, Lummox doesn't have much but it does have the fucking f-word. You're going to have to try harder if you want to shock me."

The exchange had gone by so quickly that Lucas hadn't had a chance to say anything. But in the pause that followed, he stepped forward, his eyes burning hot. "Nick, you will not speak like that to my mate!"

Nick gave Lucas and Journey an unrepentant grin. "We're cool. Just wanted to make sure."

"Make sure of what?" Lucas inquired icily.

Make sure I'm good enough for you, Journey thought. She grinned back at Nick, suddenly liking him.

Nick rolled his eyes at Lucas. "Make sure she's not the fucking foreign princess they were trying to stick you with. Duh."

Fiona's sharp gaze raked over Journey's necklace and rings. "I see that you appreciate fine jewelry. I don't imagine there's much of that in Lummox."

Journey bristled at the implication of gold-digging. Her hand went protectively to her dragon pendant.

Lucas turned to the blonde woman. Journey expected him to be angry, but his voice was unexpectedly gentle. "Fiona. That is unworthy of you. Journey risked her life to save mine. She fought by my side. She took care of me day and night when I was poisoned—"

"Poisoned!" Destiny grabbed him by the arm, her soft brown eyes wide with concern. "Lucas, my God! Are you all right?"

"I am *now.* Thanks to my mate."

"Really." Shane's cold eyes fixed on Journey.

He did nothing but look at her, but she knew in her gut that she was in terrible danger. He was going to kill her, right there and then. Not even Lucas could save her. Desperately, knowing it was a useless gesture, she snatched up her backpack and flung it at him.

"What the—" Rafa exclaimed.

"Shane!" Lucas yelled. "How dare you!"

Journey stared, bewildered, as Lucas slammed Shane into the wall.

Shane didn't fight or even blink, though his ribs had to have been bruised at the very least. Instead, he addressed Journey over Lucas's shoulder. "You're a fighter. That's good. I could teach you some actual techniques some time, if you like."

The sense of danger vanished as if it had never been. Her fear gave way to curiosity. "How did you do that?" Hopefully, she asked, "Magic?"

Shane's cool blue gaze met hers, full of mysteries she was never going to solve. "Just a thing I do."

"Lucas, let go of him," Hal ordered.

Reluctantly, Lucas released his grip on Shane's shoulders. Then he turned to address the entire room. "Journey is my mate and I love her. If you must doubt someone's worthiness, doubt mine."

His amber gaze caught and held each team member in turn until they nodded their acceptance.

Destiny broke the silence. "Sorry about the hazing. The testosterone can get pretty thick around here."

"Speak for yourself," retorted Fiona. But she turned to Journey and said, "My apologies. I just—"

"You just had to be sure," Journey said resignedly.

Hal cleared his throat. "Journey, Protection, Inc. would like to invite you to lunch to make up for being a bunch of macho idiots. Right, guys?"

A hasty chorus of assent rose. The next thing Journey knew, she and Lucas were sitting down with the rest of Protection, Inc., eating some of the best order-in sandwiches she'd had in her life.

Hal called his mate, Ellie, and she joined them halfway through. To Journey's relief, either Ellie didn't haze or Hal had warned her not to, because she was nothing but sweet to Journey. But so was everyone else. The hazing had been nerve-rattling, but she wasn't angry at them. They'd only been trying to look out for Lucas.

After lunch, the team said their good-byes and left. On their way out, Fiona gave Lucas his gold pistol, Destiny gave him his car keys, and Rafa gave him his apartment keys and a wink. Finally, they were left alone.

"I like your team," Journey said.

Lucas gave a wry chuckle. "You're very forgiving. I should have warned you about them. They did something similar to Ellie. But I thought that was only because they care so much about Hal."

"They care that much about you."

"I know," Lucas said, his voice roughening. "I know that now."

Journey followed him out of the conference room where they'd had lunch. She thought he was going out, but he instead went into another office and sat down in front of an impressive-looking computer.

"Want to make sure that honorless thief you knew in Lummox never harms any woman again?" Lucas asked.

"Yes, of course," Journey replied. "I did report him to the police. But no one knew his real name."

"I don't need to know his real name." Lucas worked on the computer for several hours. Journey watched over his shoulder as he searched a series of police databases, occasionally asking her for more information or showing her photos. Every time, she had to regretfully shake her head.

Apologetically, Lucas said, "I'm not very skilled with computers. I didn't use them at all until I was eighteen. I'll give it another hour. If I can't find him by then, I'll ask one of the others for help. Not Hal. He didn't grow up with computers either."

Half an hour later, Journey spotted her ex. "That's him!"

"Ah-ha." Lucas pulled up another screen of information. "He's moved on to Montana. And he hasn't gotten away with everything; he's in jail for credit card fraud. Let's make certain he stays there."

Journey watched him write a brief report tying her ex-boyfriend to multiple reports of theft in different states under different names, then email it to an FBI agent with a note that at least one of his victims would be willing to testify against him.

Lucas shut down the computer and stood up. "There. That should keep him in prison for another next ten years."

Amazed, Journey exclaimed, "How did you do that? The police told me it would be impossible to track him down!"

"The Lummox police?"

"Yeah." Realizing what he meant, she added, "Of course they didn't find him. They don't know how to catch anything but stray cows. I should have called the FBI—they'd have nabbed him years ago. I was so naïve!"

Lucas put his hand on her shoulder. "Nobody else thought of contacting the FBI, either. He seems to target women in small towns for exactly that reason—they report him to their local police stations, and the report never goes any farther. But he won't get away this time."

She thought of Duke Constantine, who had manipulated Lucas and Raluca for years. They were finally free, and he was locked away in a dungeon. "Better late than never."

As they left the office room, she added, "Nice job with the computer. I don't know what you mean, saying you're not good with them."

"Fiona taught me to use the system here. But I studied hard."

"It paid off. Competence is very sexy."

Lucas looked pleased as a cat with a saucer of cream. "Would you like to see the rest of what we do?"

"Absolutely!"

He showed her more offices, a private gym, and a room full of weapons and protective gear. Journey stared at the array of guns. It sank in for the first time that Lucas's job was putting himself in harm's way.

As if he had read her thought, he said, "I have never been wounded while working here. I promise you, I am much better at being a bodyguard than I am at using a computer."

"I believe you. Besides, there's the mate bond. If you ever do get in the sort of trouble where you need me, that voice will start yelling in my ear and I'll come running."

She expected Lucas to protest that he didn't need protection and if he did get in trouble, she wouldn't be able to help him anyway. Instead, he simply said, "Good. But in that case, you should take Shane up on his offer to teach you self-defense."

Journey hesitated, recalling that chilling sense of danger. "Was he serious about that? I don't know…"

"He was serious. If you're not comfortable with him, any one of us could teach you. But Shane doesn't often make such offers, and you could not learn from anyone better." After a moment, Lucas added, "He taught me as well. He doesn't teach like Grand Duke Vaclav, or I would not suggest it."

"Oh." Journey thought about it. "Okay, I'll do it."

It's a whole new world, she thought. Martial arts lessons from a terrifying panther shifter bodyguard. Meeting Lucas's friends. Living with Lucas. Being in love. She didn't have to move around constantly to find new areas to explore and new things to learn.

He drove her back to his apartment in the sleek sports car that Destiny had left parked in the Protection, Inc. garage. She had expected his apartment to resemble his room in the palace, lavishly decorated with antique furniture, marble, and gold. Instead, it was spare and modern, even austere.

"Do you like this style or did you just not intend to stay for very long?" Journey asked.

"Both," Lucas replied. "I may acquire a few more possessions now that I'm not expecting to be dragged away at any moment."

"You should put up some pictures."

"Perhaps you could help me select some," Lucas suggested. "It's your home too, now."

The apartment reminded her of photos she'd seen of homes in Japan. She'd always wanted to go there. "Cities around the world?"

"Yes. I would like that." Then he beckoned her farther in.

His bedroom was in the same style, but the bed looked soft and luxurious. Late afternoon sunlight filtered in through a window, dappling the white cover with gold.

Journey looked at the bed, then at Lucas. The air between them felt suddenly charged with sexual heat. Without even having been touched, her nipples hardened within the silk cups of her bra, and she felt herself starting to get wet.

Lucas had dressed in a tailored suit for the last leg of their trip back, and looked extraordinarily handsome in it. His black suit jacket made his hair even brighter by contrast. He was all covered up, with none of his dragonmarks showing and little of his gold. All she could see was the rings on his fingers and the chain around his throat, half-concealed by his shirt collar. She wanted to tear the suit off him, touch the heat of his naked body, press her skin to his—

"Outside of the jewelry shop, you made me a promise." His voice was low, deepened with desire.

"I remember." Journey knew what he wanted, and she didn't mind delaying her own desires a little while. "Sit down and watch."

Lucas sat on the bed, his amber eyes intent on her.

Journey began to strip for him. She lifted one foot to the bed and unbuckled her shoe, then switched feet and did it again. She'd never thought of her feet as a sexy part of her body, but Lucas leaned over and caressed first one, then the other, running his finger along the arch as if it was some fine piece of sculpture. His touch made her whole body tingle.

She was wearing a Brandusan blouse with crossed ribbons in the front. Journey undid the knots, then offered Lucas the end of one ribbon. He held it in his long-fingered hands, then gave it a tug. The blouse fell open. She undid her bra and shrugged her shoulders, and both blouse and bra slipped to the floor.

Lucas drew in his breath. Journey could almost feel his gaze on her skin, hot as summer sunlight, as he looked from her breasts to her belly to her dragon pendant. She loved the way he looked at her.

"You're so beautiful," he said. "Let me see the rest of you."

She stepped out of her long skirt, leaving it in an indigo puddle on the floor, and then rolled off her panties. Journey stood nude before him, adorned with the jewelry he'd given her. A gold chain wound up her left forearm, emerald earrings dangled from her ears, rings sparkled on her fingers, and his dragon pendant nestled in the hollow of her throat. It was as if he was already touching her, everywhere that his gifts to her rested, warm against her skin.

"You are my most precious treasure," he whispered.

"And you're mine," Journey replied.

She couldn't bear to stand apart from him any more. Journey dropped down to the bed, reaching out, desperate to touch him. He caught her in his arms and kissed her. The heat of his mouth and body made her feel like she was burning up. But it was the kind of fire that only made her want more heat.

She tugged off his suit jacket and fumbled with his shirt buttons, impatient to touch his skin. Caught up in her urgency, Lucas jerked at his shirt as well. Buttons popped off and went rolling across the floor. He tossed his shirt down to follow them, and then his shoes and pants.

Then they were naked together, stripped of all but their gold. The scars across Lucas's chest had healed and gone, leaving nothing but his glittering dragonmarks. The heat from his body and the spicy scent of him lit a fire in her. They fell to the bed together, kissing and touching, frantic with desire. Everything about him dizzied her: the hot touch of his hands, the cool caress of his chains, the taste of his mouth, the smoothness of his skin, the hard rod of his erection pressing against her thighs.

Journey ran her tongue over the dragonmarks on his shoulder, following its pattern. Lucas inhaled sharply, his hands clenching on her shoulders.

"Are they sensitive?" she asked.

"Ah—yes," he managed. "Yes, a little."

"Only a little?" she teased.

He gave her a plaintive glance. "Don't stop."

She returned her attention to them, kissing and licking as if she was painting them on anew, enjoying Lucas's reactions. When she finished tracing the dragonmarks on his belly, she wriggled downward to taste him in another sensitive area, licking around his shaft, then taking him in her mouth. Lucas gasped, his eyes falling shut, his fists clenched.

"I—" he gasped. "I—Please—"

Those were the last coherent words Lucas got out. She sucked hard and flicked her tongue over the swollen head, and then he was unable to do anything but moan. His whole body was shaking, helpless in the grip of sensation. Journey loved the clean taste of him, the touch on her tongue of soft skin over rock-hard flesh, and seeing how she could make someone so cool lose control.

He suddenly pushed her away. Startled, Journey looked down at him as he gasped for breath, visibly trying to collect himself.

"Sorry," he said at last. "I was about to come. I didn't want to finish so soon. I would've told you to stop, but I couldn't get any words out."

Journey grinned. "I think I'm flattered."

"You should be."

Then Lucas pounced, tumbling her over on to her back. He kissed her breasts, his tongue licking at her nipples like a caress of flame, and then Journey was the one to moan. She moaned again when he reached down between her legs and touched her slick heat, rubbing at her sensitive folds and swollen clit, sending her to the brink of orgasm.

Then he raised himself over her. His face was flushed, his eyes bright as gold. She opened her legs to him, eager to have him inside her. He thrust himself into her, making her gasp with pleasure. His fingers were still on her clit as he thrust inside her, stimulating her everywhere. Journey moaned, then screamed, as out of control as Lucas had been a moment ago.

She felt the hot jet as he came inside her, and then her own climax transported her. For a timeless moment, she knew nothing but sheer ecstasy, bright as the sun. Then she slowly drifted back to reality, and found herself clasped tight in Lucas's warm embrace.

I'm home, Journey thought. *Wherever I travel, wherever we go, this will always be my home. Here, in Lucas's arms.*

His hair clung to his forehead, darkened with sweat. Journey's was curling into damp ringlets. He lifted his hand and idly toyed with one, twisting it around his finger. For a while they kissed and stroked each other's skin, enjoying the afterglow.

Then Lucas spoke. "Before I left, Hal was talking about expanding the operations of Protection, Inc."

"Uh-huh…?" Journey said lazily. It seemed an odd subject to bring up immediately after making love.

"For international assignments."

That caught her interest. "Oh!"

Lucas smiled. "I thought you'd like that. I was thinking that I could take those, and if it was possible for you to come with me, you could explore while I work. We might not be able to see each other often—or at all—while I'm on assignment. But once it's done, we could stay for a while afterward."

"That's fine," she assured him. "I'm used to traveling alone. I'll just save the best areas for when you can join me."

"That would suit me as well." Lucas kissed her, then asked, "Would you ever wish to visit Lummox? I know you don't like it. But you have family there. And you've already met mine…"

A few months ago, Journey would have recoiled in horror at the thought of returning to Lummox. Now, she said, "Yeah, you should meet my parents. And the rest of the town. It'll be fun to introduce you to everyone who called me stupid and naïve and all that stuff."

"Wear *all* your jewelry," Lucas suggested, smiling.

"I will. And I'd love to go back to Brandusa some day. Though I don't know if *you* would."

"I think I'll enjoy it more as a tourist." Lucas touched her dragon pendant, then trailed his fingers upward to her lips. "I'll fly you there on dragonback. In the summer, when we can taste the forbidden fruit."

A NOTE FROM ZOE CHANT

Thank you for reading *Defender Dragon!* I hope you enjoyed it. If you're starting the series here and would like to know more about Protection, Inc. the first book is *Bodyguard Bear*, the second is *Defender Dragon*, and the third is *Protector Panther*. All of those books, along with my others, are available at Amazon.com. You can find a complete list of my books at zoechant.com.

If you enjoy *Protection, Inc.,* I highly recommend Lia Silver's *Werewolf Marines (Laura's Wolf, Prisoner,* and *Partner)* and Lauren Esker's *Shifter Agents (Handcuffed to the Bear, Guard Wolf, Dragon's Luck,* and *Tiger in the Hot Zone).* All three series have hot romances, exciting action, brave heroines who stand up for their men, hunky heroes who protect their mates with their lives, and teams of shifters who are as close as families. They are all available on Amazon.

The cover of *Defender Dragon* was designed by Augusta Scarlett.

SPECIAL SNEAK PREVIEW

PROTECTOR PANTHER

PROTECTION, INC.
3

CHAPTER ONE
Catalina

Catalina Mendez strolled down the empty street at 3:00 AM, humming to herself.

It was her favorite time of day—night—well, technically day. Statistically speaking, a high percentage of bad things happened at 3:00 AM. It was a peak time for vehicle crashes, industrial accidents, medical crises, and violent crimes. For an adrenaline junkie paramedic on the late shift, it was the best and most exciting time to work, when she might actually get to save a life. It didn't hurt that Catalina was a night owl, working at peak efficiency by night and a little sleepy and slow by day.

But right now, she wasn't just at peak efficiency. She was *wired*. She'd just flown back from the small European country of Loredana, where she'd been working with Paramedics Without Borders to help restore emergency services after a catastrophic earthquake.

Her return trip had been a catastrophe all by itself. Her best friend and fellow paramedic Ellie McNeil had been supposed to pick her up at the airport, but her flight had been delayed, then canceled, then restored so many times that Catalina had finally texted Ellie to forget about it. Catalina was perfectly capable of taking a taxi whenever the hell her flight got in. Which had been originally scheduled for 6:00 PM on Wednesday, but turned out to be 2:00 AM on Friday.

By the time the plane took off, she'd drunk several gallons of coffee to make sure she didn't doze off in the airport and miss her flight. Then she figured she might as well drink some more, since she was already wide awake. By the time the plane touched down in Santa Martina, she'd worked up a pretty good caffeine rush. Her nerves tingled with excited anticipation that something exciting and important might happen at any second.

That was when she discovered that her luggage had been routed to Singapore. Which was certainly exciting and important, but not in a good way. She picked up her purse, which was all she'd taken on the plane, and made her way to the taxi stand.

As the taxi headed toward her home, she realized how little she wanted to go there. It would be boring. And lonely. She couldn't even reunite with her cats—Ellie had taken them while Catalina was away. Her bed would be cold and empty without any kitties to cuddle.

Thoughts of Ellie and bed led to thoughts of the man who now shared Ellie's bed, hot bodyguard Hal Brennan. And the other hot bodyguards at Hal's private security company, Protection, Inc. Ellie had promised to introduce Catalina to them when she got back from Loredana. She'd even offered to send photos, but though Catalina had been impressed with the pics of Hal, she'd declined to look at the ones of the single guys. She'd meet them in person eventually, and she liked being surprised.

The taxi stopped at a red light. Catalina recognized the silhouette of a towering office building a couple blocks ahead. It had been in one of the photos Ellie had emailed her, of her and Hal standing in front of Protection, Inc.

"Let me off here," Catalina said impulsively. "It's walking distance from my home."

The taxi driver craned his head at her. "Are you sure? It's a pretty long walk. And it's the middle of the night."

"I'm sure," she said.

Catalina paid him and stepped out on to the empty street. Sure, no one would be at Protection, Inc. But she'd at least get to take a closer look at the place she'd heard so much about. And she needed to burn off some energy before she went home, or she'd never get to sleep. Besides, night was the best time to walk around the city. The air was cool, the sky was a pretty purple-orange with light spill, and you never knew what might happen.

A vision of her mother popped into her mind as she walked down the street.

Walking alone at night in the city! Mom's remembered voice was loud in her ears. *You could be robbed! You could be murdered! You could witness a murder, like your poor friend Ellie! Why are you always so reckless?*

It's a good neighborhood, mom, Catalina replied to the voice in her head, echoing real conversations they'd had a thousand times over. *I'm not reckless. I'm just not afraid.*

You should be, Mom scolded. *Ever since you were a little girl, you haven't known the meaning of fear. I pray every night that when you do find out, it won't be too late.*

The street was empty and silent. As Catalina came closer to the towering office building that housed Protection, Inc., she saw that she was approaching a dark alley.

Normally she would have walked right past it. What were the odds that a mugger was lurking at a deserted street on the unlikely chance that someone would walk straight past his lurking area—especially when every woman Catalina had ever met, even her brave friend Ellie, would cross the street to avoid that alley?

But tonight Catalina hesitated. An odd feeling made her stomach clench and her palms tingle.

Oh, no, she thought, dismayed. *I spent months living in a tent in a disaster zone, and now I get sick?*

Then she recognized the feeling. It wasn't one she felt often, but she knew what it was. It was fear.

She stopped to take stock, wondering what had made her feel afraid. Some little thing in the environment, too subtle for her register consciously, must have signaled that something was wrong. Something was dangerous.

Catalina took a step to the side, meaning to cross the street. She wasn't *completely* reckless. If an action seemed both dangerous and pointless, she wouldn't take it.

A man staggered out of the alley, fetched up hard against the wall of the nearest building, and slid down to the ground.

Catalina ran to him. On her way, she took a quick peek into the alley to make sure the scene was safe before she entered it. That was the part of the paramedic test she'd almost flunked, but it was second nature now. She couldn't see all the way into the alley, but what she did see was empty and still, with nothing stirring but a few discarded candy wrappers in the light breeze. There was no obvious danger, no pursuing muggers or smoke or sparking electrical wires, so she was free to tend to her patient.

See? She told the mom-in-her-head. *Not reckless!*

Catalina knelt by the man's side, giving his body a quick visual scan before she did a more detailed examination. His eyes were closed. He was tall and muscular, but lean rather than bulky. His short black hair looked soft as a cat's fur. He wore dark jeans and a white T-shirt spotted with fresh blood. More blood ran down his handsome face from a cut at his temple. His chest was moving evenly, and when she bent over him, she couldn't hear any sounds that indicated breathing difficulties. His skin seemed pale, but it was difficult to tell in the hard white glare of the street lights.

Airway: good. Breathing: good. Visible bleeding: not severe. He wasn't likely to drop dead in the next few seconds, so she'd call 911 to get the ambulance on its way before she resumed her assessment.

She opened her purse and pulled out her cell phone, then stared at it in dismay. It was her phone from Loredana, which wouldn't work in the US. She must have accidentally packed her regular phone in her suitcase. Which was in Singapore.

"Dammit!"

Her patient woke as if she'd fired a gun in the air. His body jerked, he sucked in a sudden breath, and his eyes flew open. They were blue as ice, and they fixed on her with an unsettling intensity.

"Who are you?" he demanded.

Level of consciousness: alert and responsive, Catalina thought.

She spoke in the soothing tones she always used on trauma victims. "I'm a paramedic. Is it all right if I help you?"

Legally, she had to ask permission before she did anything to anyone. Almost all of her patients automatically said yes.

The man patted his hip, then his shoulder. His eyes narrowed in a quick flicker of dismay. "I've lost my weapons. And I can't—" He broke off, looking frustrated. "I can't protect you. So no. I don't give you permission to treat me. Get out of here."

He struggled to get up, but only managed to get as far as propping himself on his elbows. More blood ran down his face. He clearly wasn't going anywhere.

"Why don't you lie back down?" Catalina suggested, turning up the soothing. "Just let me take a look at you."

"No." Most men raised their voices when they were angry or upset, but this man lowered his. It was more forceful than if he'd yelled.

"I'm a paramedic," Catalina repeated. Sometimes trauma victims were too shocked or disoriented to take in what she said the first time. "I can help you. Can you tell me what happened?"

He might be a trauma victim, but he wasn't disoriented. Those ice-blue eyes of his seemed to look right through her, as if he knew things about her that even she didn't. "If you're a paramedic, then you need my consent before you treat me. I'm not giving it. Take your phone and go. Once you're in a safe place, call—"

"That phone doesn't work in America," she interrupted him.

The man let out an exasperated breath. He again tried to get up, and again failed.

"Why can't you stand up?" Catalina asked. "Are you dizzy? Or is something wrong with your legs?"

"Both," he muttered, sounding reluctant to admit it. "I've been drugged. They ambushed me with a tranquilizer rifle."

"With a *tranquilizer rifle?*"

She'd once treated a woman who'd been the victim of friendly fire from zookeepers trying to take down an escaped capybara. Catalina had never heard of a capybara before, but it turned out to be a guinea pig the size of a sheep. It had been one of her all-time favorite calls. But that tranquilizer dart hadn't caused dizziness and paralysis, it had immediately knocked the woman unconscious. And who would use one for an ambush? Criminal... veterinarians?

Then Catalina realized the important part of what he'd let slip. "If you've been drugged, it's the same as if you were unconscious. I can assume that you *would* consent to treatment if you were in your right mind. So settle down. I just want to check you for life-threatening injuries."

His eyebrows rose in disbelief, as if it was the first time in his life that anyone had had the nerve to stand up to him. Then he took a deep breath, seeming to concentrate.

Her stomach clenched. Her palms tingled. Her heart began to pound. Nothing about the man had changed, but she suddenly knew he was dangerous. Very dangerous. Lethal. She had to run—she had to save herself—

The phone fell from her hand, the screen shattering. She scrambled to her feet, stumbling backward, desperate to get away.

But he hasn't threatened me, she thought. *He hasn't attacked me.*

He was still sprawled on the ground, bleeding, his gaze locked on hers. Deadly. Terrifying.

He's injured. He can't walk. He needs help.

All her instincts screamed at her to run. She was gasping, her pulse thundering in her ears, sweat pouring down her face and back. She'd never been so scared in her entire life.

Never abandon a patient.

It was the hardest thing she'd ever done, but Catalina took a step forward. Then another step. Then she dropped back down on her knees beside him.

Her terror vanished as if it had been switched off. The man rested his head on his arms, exhaustion etching lines around his strong features.

"I don't believe this," he muttered. "I hit you with both barrels. I laid it on so hard, I wore myself out! How are you still here?"

She stared at him. "You did that on purpose? How?"

"Practice." He raised his head. His intense gaze again fixed on her, but now she felt no fear. He had beautiful eyes. They were an astonishingly clear blue, like an early morning sky, fringed with thick black lashes.

"I've got some very bad people after me. You could get caught in the crossfire if you stay with me. But since you were playing hooky when God gave out fear..." As if against his will, he gave her an ironic smile. It transformed the hard angles of his face, making her notice again how good-looking he was. "If you can help me get up and walk a block, I can get us both into a building. Once we're inside, we'll be safe. I have friends I can call."

As an afterthought, he added, "I'll give you permission to examine me then. I know you're dying to check me out."

She couldn't tell if he was making a double entendre or a statement of fact. Strange guy. Strange hot guy who'd been ambushed with a tranquilizer rifle and could terrify you just by looking you in the eyes. Strange brave guy who preferred sacrificing himself to putting a stranger at risk.

Catalina crouched low. "Put your arm around my shoulders."

"I know the drill." He propped himself up on his left arm and put his right arm around her shoulders. It was warm, not cold with shock. Having his arm around her made her feel oddly safe and secure. As if he was protecting her, though he couldn't even walk.

She gripped his right wrist, unable to help noticing that he had amazing biceps. Amazing arms in general. Even his wrist was thick with muscle. Strange, totally ripped guy.

Strange sexy guy who knew unusual things. He knew how to do an assisted walk, and he knew the laws of consent for treatment.

"Are you a paramedic?" she asked, wrapping her left arm around his waist. He was warm all over.

He shook his head, struggling to get his legs under him. "I mean, yes, I am. But that's just a qualification, not my job. I'm—I *was*—a PJ. That's—"

"Air Force pararescue. Special Ops combat search and rescue," Catalina filled in. Quoting a poster she'd seen, she added, "Because sometimes even Navy SEALs have to call 911."

"That's right." His breath came harsh in her ear. He couldn't seem to move his legs at all, though she could feel his attempts through the tensing and flexing of his other muscles against her body. But though he thought bad guys could descend on them at any second, his voice and expression remained calm. "Did you ever want to be one?"

"Yeah, but they don't take women." Then she stared at him. "How'd you know?"

"You've got the right stuff. Mentally, I mean." Then he let out a frustrated breath and stopped struggling to move. "I hope you've got the right stuff physically, too, because we can't do an assisted walk. My legs are completely paralyzed. You'll have to drag me. Or I could give you the code to the building. It's only a block away. You could go in and call for help—"

"Forget it," she replied. "I'm not leaving you."

He smiled, but not the same amused, catlike smile she'd seen before.

This one held infinite depths of sadness and regret over its pleasant surface. "Never leave a fallen comrade, huh? Are you an airman? A Marine?"

"No, I've never served," Catalina replied. "And I'd rather not drag you. I don't know what kind of injuries you have. Do you know?"

"I'm not sure," he admitted. "The tranquilizer knocked me for a loop. I don't remember the fight too well. I'm not even sure exactly how I got here."

She glanced at the blood on his shirt. If he had internal injuries, she definitely shouldn't drag him. "I'll do a fireman's carry."

He gave her a doubtful glance, which didn't surprise her. He had to be over a foot taller and fifty pounds heavier than her. Then he shrugged. "Okay. Let's give it a try."

Catalina wrestled him over her shoulders, thanking her lucky stars that she'd just spent months in a disaster zone without any high-tech amenities. If it hadn't built up her strength moving heavy equipment and patients, she probably couldn't even have gotten him into position.

She stood up, careful to lift from her legs, not her back. He weighed even more than she'd imagined. Her knees cracked audibly, and she staggered.

"Easy." He laid a steadying hand on her forearm. "Find your center of gravity and settle into it."

"Thanks," she gasped, regaining her balance. "Which way?"

"Forward. I'll tell you when we get there."

She took a step forward, trying not to pitch forward under his weight. Her breath burned in her lungs, and her back and legs and neck ached. She didn't feel like she could make it five more steps, let alone an entire city block. But her other choice was dragging him over the sidewalk and maybe making his injuries worse. She took another step, and then another one.

Another step. Another.

A quarter of a block.

Her face felt hot and swollen with blood. Her back was on fire.

Another step. Another.

Half a block. Catalina felt like she was about to pass out. She could see nothing but a red haze.

"You're strong," he said quietly.

138

Hearing that from a PJ—hearing it from this man, in particular—gave her strength.

Another step.

He suddenly whipped his arm out like he was slapping something out of the air. The shift in weight nearly knocked her off her feet. As she staggered, trying to regain her balance, she saw some tiny object rolling across the sidewalk.

"Put me down and run!" he said sharply.

"No!" A pain like a needle jab pricked her arm. "Ow!"

Everything spun around her, and she hit the ground hard. Catalina couldn't so much as twitch. When she tried to speak, she found that not even her lips would move. But now she was close enough to the ground to see the tiny object on the sidewalk: a tranquilizer dart. Another one was still embedded in her arm.

The PJ dragged himself on top of her and shielded her with his body.

"Last stand," he muttered. "Funny how by the time it comes to that, you're never actually standing."

Then he glanced down at her open eyes. "Oh. Didn't realize you were still conscious. Last stand for me, I mean. I'll make sure it isn't yours."

He laid his palm down on her back. It was warm. Comforting.

Catalina's vision kept blurring and the PJ was blocking her line of sight, but she could see some figures approaching them.

"The woman's a civilian," the PJ said. His voice carried on the still air, but his tone was calm as if he was having a perfectly normal conversation. "Just an ordinary good Samaritan. Leave her here. She doesn't know anything. I didn't even tell her my name."

Another man's voice spoke. If the PJ was cool, this man was ice cold. "We know. We've been observing from a distance. And we've seen some *fascinating* things. Her resistance to your power—her general lack of fear—even her physical strength. We're certainly not leaving her. She's the perfect subject for 2.0."

There was a brief silence. Then all of the hazy figures flinched back. One let out a hoarse scream of sheer terror, then spun around and ran away. A moment later, two more followed him, stumbling and arms flailing, apparently caught in the grip of total panic.

The man with the cold voice spoke again. "I'm impressed. My operatives all underwent intensive fear-resistance training. However, I anticipated that you might get to some of them anyway. That's why I brought as many men as I did. The three I have left should be more than enough to deal with one partially paralyzed, unarmed renegade."

The PJ replied coolly, "Send them over, and we'll see about that."

"It would be interesting to see what you can manage in that state. However, in the interest of expediting this, I think I'll just give you another dose."

There was snap of fingers, then a faint *whump* of compressed air. Catalina felt the PJ whip around. His hand brushed against her shoulder as he yanked something from his side and threw it back. One of the figures yelped in pain. Then the PJ gave a long sigh and slumped down on top of her. His breathing was even and deep, his hair soft against her cheek.

The figures moved forward, coming closer and closer. Catalina blinked hard, trying to clear her vision. The name on the building in front of her swam into view. She'd collapsed right in front of Protection, Inc.

Too bad no one's home, she thought dizzily. *Right now, we could really use a bodyguard.*

Everything went black.

ZOE CHANT
COMPLETE BOOK LIST

All books are available through Amazon.com. Check my website, zoechant.com, for my latest releases.

While series should ideally be read in order, all of my books are standalones with happily ever afters and no cliffhangers. This includes books within series.

BOOKS IN SERIES

Protection, Inc.
Book 1: *Bodyguard Bear*
Book 2: *Defender Dragon*
Book 3: *Protector Panther*
Book 4: *Warrior Wolf*

Bears of Pinerock County
Book 1: *Sheriff Bear*
Book 2: *Bad Boy Bear*
Book 3: *Alpha Rancher Bear*
Book 4: *Mountain Guardian Bear*

Cedar Hill Lions
Book 1: *Lawman Lion*
Book 2: *Guardian Lion*
Book 3: *Rancher Lion*
Book 4: *Second Chance Lion*

Enforcer Bears
Book 1: *Bear Cop*

Book 2: *Hunter Bear*
Book 3: *Wedding Bear*
Book 4: *Fighter Bear*

Fire & Rescue Shifters
Book 1: *Firefighter Dragon*
Book 2: *Firefighter Pegasus*
Book 3: *Firefighter Griffin*
Book 4: *Firefighter Sea Dragon*

Glacier Leopards
Book 1: *The Snow Leopard's Mate*
Book 2: *The Snow Leopard's Baby*
Book 3: *The Snow Leopard's Home*
Book 4: *The Snow Leopard's Heart*

Gray's Hollow Dragon Shifters
Book 1: *The Billionaire Dragon Shifter's Mate*
Book 2: *Beauty and the Billionaire Dragon Shifter*
Book 3: *The Billionaire Dragon Shifter's Christmas*
Book 4: *Choosing the Billionaire Dragon Shifters*
Book 5: *The Billionaire Dragon Shifter's Baby*
Book 6: *The Billionaire Dragon Shifter Meets His Match*

Hollywood Shifters
Book 1: *Hollywood Bear*
Book 2: *Hollywood Dragon*
Book 3: *Hollywood Tiger*
Book 4: *A Hollywood Shifters' Christmas*

Honey for the Billionbear
Book 1: *Honey for the Billionbear*
Book 2: *Guarding His Honey*
Book 3: *The Bear and His Honey*

Ranch Romeos
Book 1: *Bear West*

Book 2: *The Billionaire Wolf Needs a Wife*

Rowland Lions
Book 1: *Lion's Hunt*
Book 2: *Lion's Mate*

Shifter Kingdom
Book 1: *Royal Guard Lion*
Book 2: *Royal Guard Tiger*

Shifting Sands Resort
Book 1: *Tropical Tiger Spy*
Book 2: *Tropical Wounded Wolf*

Upson Downs
Book 1: *Target: Billionbear*
Book 2: *A Werewolf's Valentine*

NON-SERIES BOOKS

Bears

A Pair of Bears
Alpha Bear Detective
Bear Down
Bear Mechanic
Bear Watching
Bear With Me
Bearing Your Soul
Bearly There
Bought by the Billionbear
Country Star Bear
Dancing Bearfoot
Hero Bear
In the Billionbear's Den
Kodiak Moment

Private Eye Bear's Mate
The Bear Comes Home For Christmas
The Bear With No Name
The Bear's Christmas Bride
The Billionbear's Bride
The Easter Bunny's Bear
The Hawk and Her LumBEARjack

Big Cats

Alpha Lion
Joining the Jaguar
Loved by the Lion
Panther's Promise
Pursued by the Puma
Rescued by the Jaguar
Royal Guard Lion
The Billionaire Jaguar's Curvy Journalist
The Jaguar's Beach Bride
The Saber Tooth Tiger's Mate
Trusting the Tiger

Dragons

The Christmas Dragon's Mate
The Dragon Billionaire's Secret Mate
The Mountain Dragon's Curvy Mate

Eagles

Wild Flight

Griffins

The Griffin's Mate
Ranger Griffin

Wolves

IF YOU LOVE ZOE CHANT, YOU'LL ALSO LOVE THESE BOOKS!

Laura's Wolf (Werewolf Marines # 1), by Lia Silver. Werewolf Marine Roy Farrell, scarred in body and mind, thinks he has no future. Curvy Laura Kaplan, running from danger and her own guilty secrets, is desperate to escape her past. Together, they have all that they need to heal. A full-length novel.

Prisoner (Werewolf Marines # 2), by Lia Silver. Werewolf Marine DJ Torres is a born rebel. Genetically engineered assassin Echo was created to be a weapon. When DJ is captured by the agency that made Echo, the two misfits find that they fit together perfectly. A full-length novel.

Partner (Werewolf Marines # 3), by Lia Silver. DJ and Echo's relationship grows stronger under fire… until they're confronted by a terrible choice. A full-length novel.

Mated to the Meerkat, by Lia Silver. Jasmine Jones, a curvy tabloid reporter, meets her match—in more ways than one—in notorious paparazzi and secret shifter Chance Marcotte. A romantic comedy novelette.

Handcuffed to the Bear (Shifter Agents # 1), by Lauren Esker. A bear-shifter ex-mercenary and a curvy lynx shifter searching for her best friend's killer are handcuffed together and hunted in the wilderness. A full-length novel.

Guard Wolf (Shifter Agents # 2), by Lauren Esker. Avery is a lone werewolf without a pack; Nicole is a social worker trying to put her life back together. When he shows up with a box of orphaned werewolf puppies, and danger in pursuit, can two lonely people find the family they've been missing in each other? A full-length novel.

Dragon's Luck (Shifter Agents # 3), by Lauren Esker. Gecko shifter and infiltration expert Jen Cho teams up with sexy dragon-shifter gambler "Lucky" Lucado to win a high-stakes poker game. Now they're trapped on a cruise ship full of mobsters, mysterious enemy agents, and evil dragons! A full-length novel.

Tiger in the Hot Zone (Shifter Agents # 4), by Lauren Esker. In her search for the truth about shifters, tell-all blogger Peri Moreland has been clashing with tiger shifter and SCB agent Noah Easton for years. Now she and Noah are on the run with an unstoppable assassin after them and a custom-made plague threatening the entire shifter world! A full-length novel.